AN ETHICAL MAN

AN ETHICAL MAN

ALANE MARK

Published in 1987 by
Academy Chicago Publishers
425 North Michigan Avenue
Chicago, IL 60611

Copyright © 1987 by Alane Mark

Printed and bound in the USA

Set by Fjord Press Typography, Seattle

No part of this book may be reproduced
in any form without the express written
permission of the publisher.

Library of Congress Cataloging-in-Publication Data

Mark, Alane.
    An ethical man.

    I. Title.
PS3563.A662E8   1986   813'.54   86-26558
ISBN 0-89733-224-5
ISBN 0-89733-223-7 (pbk.)

To P, literally an inspiration to me,
and to T, my best critic
as well as best friend.

AUTHOR'S NOTE

The author is not a lawyer and does not represent herself as one. While the interpretations of the law contained in the following are her understanding of the law as it existed in California in late winter of 1983, it is not her intention that such interpretations should be relied upon by any individual in any way.

All names and events in this novel are fictitious and any similarity to persons living or dead is purely coincidental.

San Marin Herald-Tribune, Thursday, September 12

Body of woman found in east county

The body of a woman found two days ago in the eastern portion of the county was tentatively identified today by Joseph Kolvek of this county as being that of his wife, Sharon Kolvek, 53. A Sheriff's Department spokesperson said that the condition of the body made definite identification by Mr Kolvek impossible, but that further efforts were being made to obtain a positive identification. Mrs Kolvek was reported missing by a member of the family in August of this year.

The body, which had no identification, was found in a heavily wooded and isolated area of the county not far from the Kolvek's vacation home. A survey of area residents and property tax rolls eventually led the Sheriff's Office to contact Mr Kolvek, and this contact led to the tentative identification.

The Sheriff's Office said that the deceased had suffered a head wound but declined to speculate on the cause or time of death. No family members were available for comment.

Besides her husband, Joseph, Sharon Kolvek is survived by her two daughters, Mrs Elaine Morris and Mrs Susan Jordan; a son, Thomas, and several grandchildren.

Joseph Kolvek is a prominent businessman in the community and is the owner of Kolvek Construction Co. His recent projects include the Pier Tower and the San Rafael High School.

1

"Mr Randall!"

He had almost made it to the escalator, and for a minute he considered ignoring the call. But one more delay was not going to make much difference to his schedule, which had already been wrecked, first by a five a.m. call from a panicky client and then from a jumble of late court calls and an emergency jail visit.

Jim Randall plastered a smile on his face and turned. The smile became genuine when he saw Anna, Judge Tessam's clerk, hurrying down the hallway toward him. She was still new to her job; the sight of her earnest face struck a responsive chord in him. Seventeen years ago these courthouse halls had intimidated him too.

"You're moving pretty fast for this late on a Friday afternoon," he said. She took a moment to catch her breath and then smiled back at him.

"I've got a message from your secretary,

Mr Randall. She called while you were in chambers with the judge. I kept my eye out for you, but I guess you left the one time I was away from my desk."

"Isn't that always the way? Listen, I appreciate your coming after me." He was doubly glad he had stopped when she called him. She really did not have to run after him like that. He'd have to put her on the office Christmas list.

Anna watched for a moment as he swung off toward the public phones. She couldn't help liking Randall, even when he came charging into the courthouse with papers to be filed five minutes before closing on a Friday afternoon. Most of the clerks liked him, even though some people said his manner —always friendly, never condescending— was carefully cultivated to get extra attention for him. Anna preferred to believe it just came naturally to him. She liked his smile and his warm gray eyes. And his continual— losing—battle of the waistline only added to his charm, in her opinion. She couldn't help envying his secretary, to say nothing of his wife.

Randall walked to the phone, wondering why Sally wanted him to call her. His office was only two blocks from the courthouse. It really didn't make much sense to stop and call first. But in the seven years Sally had worked for him he had learned not to second guess her. Obediently he stuck his coin in the slot and dialed.

"Mr Randall's office."

"Sally, hi, it's me. What's up?"

"Oh, hi, Jim. I just wanted to ask you to come straight back to the office if you can. Mr Eden is here to see you, with one of his clients. I told him you were in court and I didn't know when you were coming back, but I said he was welcome to wait here."

"I see," he said, although he did not. Sally never made appointments for him; a secretary could never know when a criminal defense lawyer would return from court. Today was a case in point. His discovery motion had only taken fifteen minutes, but by the luck of the draw he was last on the calendar. He had had to answer the calendar call at two o'clock and then sit through eight other cases before his was heard.

Anyway, Eden's office was only a couple of blocks away. Why couldn't he have waited there 'til Randall called him? Randall's curiosity began to simmer.

"What's it all about, do you know?"

After a short pause, Sally said, "Not exactly." He waited for her to go on but she was silent. She must have had some idea of the problem or she would not have made these arrangements. The matter was probably highly confidential and she didn't want to discuss it on the 'phone, since it was a fact of life in his criminal-law practice that the phones were intermittently bugged. Of course it was strictly illegal but on occasion the law enforcement people had been known to risk the minimal penalties: once they knew where to look they could usually find a way to get the same information legally and use it in court.

"Okay, Sally. Tell him I'm on my way."

He hefted his briefcase and headed down the escalator and out the courthouse door. As he walked briskly toward his office, he automatically smiled and nodded at acquaintances, but his mind was on other things. He gave only slight attention to a young woman wearing a tank top, short shorts and little else, although he did look twice at an aging Southern belle in rouge, long gloves, jewels, ruffles and a wide picture hat. He had a feeling that this unexpected meeting was going to interfere with his weekend plans; he was already thinking about ways to break the news to Kay that they wouldn't be able to take the kids to visit their grandparents up the coast. Maybe he could get tickets to whatever was playing Saturday night at the Shakespeare Festival. He himself was not crazy about Shakespeare, but Kay loved the plays. So that should help to compensate for her ruined weekend, although he intended to leave it to her to break the news to the children. She was used to making last minute changes; it had been a way of life for her ever since she had gone on their honeymoon ahead of him while he stayed at the office to write an emergency appeal brief.

But maybe he was jumping the gun. Maybe Sally's instincts were wrong for once and this was not an emergency and Kay and the kids would not be disappointed after all. But as he reached for the doorknob he realized with a pang of guilt that he hoped Sally was right.

He almost knocked Bill Eden down as he opened the door. Eden was pacing the floor of the reception room in a highly nervous state. The ashtray was piled with butts. Randall looked at Sally, who hated cigarette smoke.

"Jim," Eden said, "I want you to meet Joseph Kolvek."

The other man in the room, who had been sitting quietly on the couch, stood up. Kolvek was a compact man with very short salt-and-pepper hair and cool blue eyes. As they shook hands, Randall noticed the man's strength. Kolvek was sizing him up, too: Randall was well aware that his big, shaggy teddy bear look did not conform to the general image of a sharp criminal lawyer. But he believed his looks were an asset. Many witnesses were fooled by his warmth into forgetting that bears had claws.

"Glad to meet you, Mr Kolvek. Listen, if you and Bill will just be patient a few more minutes, I'd like to run into my office for a minute and unload my briefcase and talk to Sally. Won't take any time at all."

He went into the office with Sally at his heels. She closed the door behind her and handed him a newspaper clipping before he had a chance to ask her anything. "Body of Woman Found in East County." He read it carefully and then looked up at Sally, "Oh," he said. "*That* Joseph Kolvek."

"The name rang a bell when Mr Eden called the first time, so I went to the paper and found this. So when he called back later and you still weren't back, I decided he'd better come here and wait for you."

Sally certainly had the right instincts. Kolvek of Kolvek Construction could pay fees without strain, never an insignificant consideration. Besides, he was better off in Randall's office where Sally could keep the press at bay than anywhere else. And then, most importantly, this might be a homicide case. Most top criminal defense lawyers didn't deal much with violent crime, simply because people with a tendency to violence rarely had any money. It was white collar crime that paid—fraud, embezzlement, narcotics. Randall's practice was top-heavy with these kinds of cases, which could certainly be interesting, but were not as challenging and stimulating as crimes of emotion. Murder and sex cases were draining and they could cause burnout, but they provided a change of pace and got the adrenaline flowing. He felt rested and wide-awake already. He settled down behind his desk.

"Okay, Sally, send 'em in."

Out of politeness, Randall let Eden begin to speak first. He usually seized control of the conversation from the outset, since one of the first rules of criminal practice was to let the client know that he should listen only to his attorney. But that sort of thing could certainly wait until Kolvek decided whether he even wanted to retain Randall. The case seemed odd already: Kolvek was much calmer than his lawyer. It was Eden who seemed to be crying out for assurance.

"Mr Kolvek here has been my client for about twenty years," he said. "We have always advised him on various aspects of business law, but now he seems to have a problem that's out of our field. We don't think this is going to turn into a real problem for him, but we decided the best thing would be to consult an expert, and of course that's you."

"I appreciate that, Bill," Randall said. "I saw a newspaper item; I know what you're referring to. And I agree with you. It's best to go right ahead: it saves a lot of grief when you can just nip things in the bud." He uncapped his pen. "Now, Mr Kolvek, what's your full name?"

"Joseph William Kolvek."

"Any AKA's? Other names you're known by?"

"No."

"Place and date of birth?"

"August 24, 1930. Battle Creek, Michigan."

"Any military experience?"

"Three years in the army."

"Active duty?"

"Korea."

Randall looked up with a smile. "I guess that's active enough," he said, pleasantly. There was no response. Bill Eden was smoking again, and Kolvek looked at him imperturbably. "Okay," he said, and went on to Kolvek's home and office addresses and phone numbers, and his social security number. Then, the formalities completed, he capped his pen slowly, put it aside, and leaned back in his chair.

"Right. That's done. Now I told you I read the item in the paper. Why don't you tell me what happened? Start wherever you feel comfortable. We can always fill in background later. Right now I just want to get a feel for what you think the situation is."

Kolvek paused. Randall watched him gathering his thoughts. He had misread clients in the past, of course, often with unfortunate results, but here he couldn't get any reading at all. Maybe Kolvek's rocklike exterior covered only a granite interior and there wasn't anything to read. But it was something to think about if Randall got the case. It was vital to know a client's stress points.

"My wife left me last August, about six

weeks ago. She didn't leave a note. I just came home from work and she wasn't there. The last time any member of the family saw her was at dinner the night before. When no one in the family heard from her after almost a week, my daughter called the police."

"Who'd she talk to over at the police department?"

"I don't know. Anyway, it was the sheriff's office -- I live just outside the city limits. They sent two deputies over. Elaine got hysterical, and she ended up accusing me of murdering my wife."

"Elaine's your daughter? Was she close to her mother?"

"Not really. Elaine doesn't so much love her mother as she hates me." Kolvek might have been discussing a lunch date for all the emotion he showed. "But my wife had taken her bag and some clothes and the car, so there was nothing to show she hadn't just left of her own accord. So they let it go at that."

"Then three days ago some kids found a body in the foothills. The kids were out looking for arrowheads and they found this body in a ditch. I have a vacation place there, just a cabin. It's very isolated — not many people go through that area of the woods. The body was pretty far gone. The sheriffs up there checked around with the local residents and got some names off the property tax rolls. They came across my name and one of the deputies who talked to me in August happened to be in the station. My wife was still reported as missing.

"So when he called me I said that she was all right as far as I knew, but I hadn't heard from her. So they drove me up there yesterday. That body was in pretty bad shape — we've had a wet summer, you know, and it's been pretty warm — Not much left of the face. I told them I couldn't be sure. But the rings looked familiar. Now I gather they're checking with Sharon's dentist. That's all I know."

He sat back abruptly and folded his arms. He obviously believed that he had said everything there was to say. That was probably a very long speech for Kolvek, but there were a lot of gaps in the story. Randall was about to zero in on these, when he noticed that Bill Eden was looking a little pale. He had seemed restless when Kolvek had talked about the condition of the body. Eden's was the world of business law, where throats were cut figuratively only and the stains on the carpet were inkstains.

"Bill, your secretary is probably wondering what happened to you, isn't she? Mr Kolvek and I can manage from here, if you'd like to get back to the office. I'll get in touch if we have any problems."

They all knew that Eden's secretary would have gone home an hour ago. It was almost six. But no one said anything.

"Well, I should be getting back," Eden

said gratefully. He stood up and Randall followed him to open his office door for him. Sally was still at her desk. After Eden had left, she said, "I thought I'd just stick around for a while in case you needed anything. I called Kay and told her you'd be home late."

He looked quickly at his watch; he'd forgotten to tell Kay he would miss dinner. "Thanks a lot, Sally," he said. But she knew how much he appreciated her thoughtfulness. He went back into his office, determined to loosen Kolvek up a little.

He opened his credenza to reveal a small bar. "Can I get you something to drink, Mr Kolvek? We've got all the usual. Scotch? Vodka?"

Kolvek shook his head. Randall looked at him for a moment.

"Well, why don't I just open a beer for you," he said, "in case you change your mind."

He popped open a cold can of Budweiser and put it near the client on a coaster. He poured himself a small shot of bourbon and settled down again behind the desk, where he rapidly skimmed his notes.

"Now. Did your daughter follow up her initial accusation?"

"Not that I know of."

"Do you know why she dropped it?"

"No."

"Maybe she decided Mrs Kolvek had just left home after all?"

"I have no idea."

Randall was becoming fed up with these monosyllabic replies. What would Kolvek do if his lawyer just sat there and stared back at him? But that would be childish. He had to appeal to him somehow.

"Mr Kolvek," he said slowly, "we haven't discussed fees, but as you can imagine, my time is expensive. I don't know whether you're trying to save time and money by giving me these brief replies. If that's the case, I have to tell you that that approach is going to consume more time than if you gave me full answers. If I'm going to give you competent representation, I have to know all the details. I know you are not the kind of person who likes to spill his guts to a complete stranger, but if you make me drag everything out of you bit by bit, we're going to be here all night. Okay?"

Kolvek stared into his eyes for a moment, and then nodded slowly and began to talk.

"My daughter Elaine made a good marriage, I suppose. Some people call it marrying old money. You know what I mean?" Randall nodded. "Right. That was about fifteen, sixteen years ago, when I was still a struggling subcontractor. Elaine was always desperate to get away from home and Don Morris was her way out. The fact that he's a womanizing drunk didn't matter to her at all.

"So naturally she's very conscious of her

social status. She hates me because I don't like to play the kind of games she plays and pretend to be something I'm not. She'd like to see me take a hard fall, but she doesn't want to do anything that will make her look bad or hurt her position, you know? If she pushed this thing about her mother too hard some of the mud might land on her. She's not my only daughter, by the way. Susan's the other one. She's got problems of her own, she doesn't want to start a lot of trouble. Naturally she wants to find out what happened to her mother, don't get me wrong. She loves her mother."

He stopped talking and, as though this long speech had dried his throat, took a swallow of beer.

"And you have one son," Randall said.

"Yes, that's right. Thomas." He made a wry face. "He'll go along with any program. If he's with Elaine, he says he thinks I killed Sharon, and if he's with me he says Elaine is a hysterical bitch. You can't count on him for anything."

Randall was a little taken aback at this abrupt disposition of Kolvek's family. Apparently he disliked them — except for Susan, possibly.

"So you thought your wife had just gone off and left you, Mr Kolvek?"

"Yes. I thought it was kind of funny that she didn't ask me for money. But new charges kept showing up on her credit cards, so naturally I thought she was all right."

"You and your wife have joint credit cards?"

"That's right."

"And charges you hadn't made kept showing up on those cards?"

"Yes. Now I think what happened was that her purse must have been stolen. You don't get actual copies of the charge slips any more, so I had no way of knowing she wasn't signing them."

"Okay. Hang on a minute." He got up and took his notes to the outer office. "Sally, I'm going to need a confidential financial authorization for Mr Kolvek to sign. Leave the addressee blank — we're going to be sending it to several places. We need information about charge slips, credit balances, bank statements and any other financial information you can think of. Okay?"

"How about medical or employment records?"

"No, not right now. We'll think about it if that becomes an issue."

"Straight signature or notarized?"

"You better make it notarized to be on the safe side."

He handed her his notes for Kolvek's social security number and other information, and she began to riffle through her authorization file for the right form. He went back to Kolvek.

"I'll need a list of all the credit cards your

wife might have had with her, so we can write to the companies and get copies of the original charge slips. That might give us a start finding out what happened to her."

Kolvek nodded. "And you'll give that information to the sheriff's office?"

"I don't know what I'll do with the information. At this point all I'm doing is trying to collect all the facts. And I'll handle things in whatever way seems most advantageous for you."

Sally tapped quickly on the door and came in with several sheets of paper. She handed him one. "I've made a note on the authorization that a duplicate has the same force and effect as the original, but I've run out several originals anyway. Banks get a little sticky about little things sometimes."

Randall checked through the authorizations. "This looks fine, Sally, thanks a lot. What we're going to do is have Mr Kolvek sign them in a little while and then you can bring in your notary stamp and witness his signature. Over the weekend Mr Kolvek is going to get together a list of his credit cards and numbers, and on Monday we'll send out some letters."

"If I could make a suggestion," Sally said. "It would be easier on everybody if Mr Kolvek just gave me the bills. Then I'll have all the information I need and I won't have to keep calling him for details."

Randall looked at Kolvek, who nodded in

agreement. After Sally left, Randall began to explain the form to his client.

"Now this form authorizes me as your attorney to ask about anything I want that has to do with your personal financial records. You sign this now as an individual because I don't see any reason to go into your business dealings right now. That might become necessary later, but we can talk about it then, if it does.

"The main thing is that this form identifies me as your attorney. So what we need to do is determine if that is what you want. Up to now I've just been gathering information from you. Now this conversation is privileged as between attorney and client, and confidential, but I haven't been retained as yet. You aren't under any obligation to retain me if you'd rather not. All you have to do is tell me you don't want me as your attorney. I'll have to bill you for my time this afternoon and that will formalize the attorney-client relationship between us, and you will be free to go wherever you want. I'll be happy to give you names of good defense lawyers, or maybe you'd rather ask Bill Eden. And that'll be that. Okay?"

Kolvek nodded.

"On the other hand, if you do decide you want me to represent you, we have to discuss fees. I don't want any misunderstandings. I'll run over the details for you now, but I'll put it all in writing so you can think about it. I usually ask for a retainer of $10,000 in a homicide investigation. That money secures my services in representing you and only you in connection with this matter. And I would expect you to pay all costs, for any traveling I might have to do, or for the possible hiring of an investigator.

"Then if charges are filed against you, you would have to pay an additional retainer to secure my services in defending you against those charges. In a full-scale murder case that second retainer could run between $50,000 and $75,000, depending on the complexity of the case and various other factors. And please remember that if you retain me in the investigative stage, you are not required to keep me as your lawyer in the court stage. As a matter of fact, you're free to drop me as your attorney at any point. You won't get back the retainer you've paid up to then, but you won't be obligated for any additional retainer. Still with me?"

Kolvek nodded again. He hadn't even blinked when the retainers were mentioned. Maybe the man was just a breathing rock.

"Okay, now we come to one last point. I'm making absolutely no guarantees about the outcome of any of these proceedings. I'm going to do my best to see to it that you don't get charged, but I can't guarantee that you won't. And if you are charged, I can't make any representations about the likelihood of a conviction or the probabilities of any jail time. At least we don't have to hassle with the death penalty, because this case doesn't fall into any of those special circumstance categories.

"I just want it clearly understood that all you're getting for your money is my best effort on your behalf. You aren't buying the outcome. A lot of clients assume that when they fork over that much money they're also buying a judge or a prosecutor. I don't know if any judges out there are on the take and I don't want to know, but if there are any, they're not in my pocket, I can tell you that for certain. I don't offer bribes and all you're getting for your money is my expertise. Understood? Okay, any questions?"

"No, I understand the fee arrangement. I definitely want you as my lawyer and the fees are acceptable to me."

"Okay, Mr Kolvek, now that we both understand what we're looking at, I'd like to depart from my usual practice in your case. We've got an unusual situation here — we don't know that there was a crime committed. And right now we don't even know if you'll be the target of an investigation. Maybe the coroner will take one look at the body and determine that your wife died of natural causes — assuming that body is your wife's. The thing is, you don't want to leave the investigation entirely in the hands of the police. You want me to watch out for your rights and put in our two cents worth whenever I think it'll do the most good. Right?"

"That's right. I told Bill Eden and I'll tell you, I don't think I've got a problem here. But even if I don't know much about other things, I know the building business, and I know the foundation is the most important part of the building. Even if nothing ever happens, I want to be sure I don't run into any problems because I made the wrong move."

"That's good thinking and it could be you'll save yourself a lot of hassle. And that reminds me — has any investigator contacted you?"

"Not since the deputy dropped me back home yesterday. Somebody did come to the house asking for me this morning. I wasn't there. He gave my housekeeper his card and said I should call him, but I haven't done it yet."

Randall glanced at the card and gave a low whistle.

"This is an investigator from the District Attorney's office. The sheriff's office didn't waste any time dumping this case."

He settled back in his chair and explained.

"The sheriff's office and the police department report to the prosecutor's office, which has the responsibility of prosecuting any alleged criminal — they're the ones who decide whether there's enough in it to go ahead. Sometimes the police stop an investigation and ask the D.A.'s office how to proceed. And other times — particularly complex cases — they just turn everything over to the D.A.'s people and let them take it on. They've got their own staff of investigators.

"This is kind of funny, though. They don't even know whether there's a case yet. I think what happened is that the sheriff's people decided this was a hot potato and they didn't want it. Usually the deputy D.A. would tell them in a case like this that they should work on it for a little while longer. But maybe we've got a deputy here who thinks it's worth it for a little publicity. This is an awfully fast transfer, though."

He thought for a moment and then swung his chair around and picked up the phone. "Let me give a quick call and see if Janis is still in his office. I know him; maybe I can find out something."

Quickly he punched out the numbers printed on the card. The phone rang repeatedly, but evidently there was no one there. He hung up and looked again at Kolvek.

"I'll try him again tomorrow. I know it's Saturday but he might just be there. And I want to tell you that I'm glad you didn't call him. From now on I don't want you talking to anyone about this case except me. And when I say anybody, I mean anybody — not just the D.A.'s office or the press, but your family, people at your office, people at the country club. Just tell them you can't comment. I know it's a temptation to give them a quick answer and get them off your back, but don't do it. It'll only cause problems later. If they pester you, refer them to me."

Even as he spoke, Randall thought to himself that if there was one client who would have no problem resisting the temptation to talk, it was Kolvek. Most people would probably not even have the nerve to bring it up to him.

"It won't be a problem for me," Kolvek said.

"Okay. Now this case is a little unusual, so I'm not going to ask you for the initial retainer at the outset. Let me look into the thing for a little while on an hourly basis. I'll charge you $250 an hour for my time and ask for a deposit for my costs. If this thing obviously isn't going to go anywhere — and that could happen — you'll only owe me the fee for my time. But if it looks like there's going to be an in-depth investigation, then the fee arrangement I outlined to you will go into effect. Okay? Then let's get your signature on these authorizations."

Sally came in with her notary paraphernalia, witnessed Kolvek's signatures and went out. Kolvek stood up.

"I do have a question," he said. "What happens next?"

"Well, if it's convenient, I'd like to come out to your house tomorrow and take a look around. Maybe we can kill two birds with one

23

stone—I'll call Janis in the morning and maybe he'll come to your place too and he can interview you at the same time. How's ten-thirty?"

Kolvek hesitated. "You work on Saturdays?"

Randall smiled. Even at the fee levels that were arranged Kolvek was going to try and watch his pennies. "Mr Kolvek, my business is not like the construction business; there isn't any extra charge for Saturdays, or any other day. I put in the necessary hours whenever they're necessary. In fact if this thing starts to heat up, I'll give you my home number so you can call me there if you need me. Any emergency after hours, just tell my answering service to put you through. They won't give you any hassle about it."

Kolvek nodded. "I'll see you tomorrow at ten-thirty," he said.

Randall saw him to the elevators and came back to the reception room.

"That's it, Sally," he said, looking at his watch. "Just six-forty-five on a Friday evening. These things never seem to come up in the middle of a slow Wednesday morning, do they?"

They walked to the elevators together.

"These information requests will have to go out first thing Monday," he said.

"I'll take care of it. And you want me to check with the coroner's office about the reports on the body?"

"God, that's right, yes. Please. They probably won't be doing the autopsy for a little while, but I want those reports as soon as they're available."

"There's a four week delay right now in getting the coroner's report even after they've done the autopsy. Should I ask them to send out the toxicology and autopsy analyses as soon as they're available and then keep checking back about the coroner's report?"

"I guess so." They reached the ground floor and began to walk toward the parking garage. "I'll go with you to your car. It's kind of late. And listen, keep this checking as casual as you can, I don't want the press to make a big deal out of Kolvek hiring a top-flight criminal lawyer."

It was true that whenever prosecutors or probation officers saw Randall's name down as defense counsel they automatically assumed there was more to the case than they might have thought, and started playing hardball even when the case was patently in the minor leagues. Randall had had to stop handling misdemeanor cases because of this, some time ago.

They reached her car. She unlocked it and he glanced into the back seat before she got in.

"And line up Jenny for me, will you? I want to see her as soon as she's free next week."

"Right. I'll try over the weekend," Sally

said. Sometimes the investigator could be a little hard to track down during the week.

"Tell Sol I'm sorry for keeping you, okay? And thanks."

Sally shrugged. "It's been a long day for you," she said.

"Boy, tell me about it. I think I'll stop at Kelley's Bar on the way home."

He lifted his hand in farewell and went back to the elevators, smiling. The only tab he ran at Kelley's was for quarters and the only shots were taken on the air hockey game at the bar. Randall was addicted to the game; it seemed to loosen him up after a hard day more than a couple of drinks would. Friends of his had been known to cross to the other side of the street if they spotted him on the way to Kelley's; he was not above hijacking people to play against him. He played every bit as hard as he worked.

THE THRIFT SOCIETY
"Helping People to Help Themselves"

RECEIPT

DATE: August 9

FROM: Joseph Kolvek

ADDRESS: 13127 Reyna Way
Racine, California

PICK UP: 27 boxes clothes, shoes, accessories, and miscellaneous

Thank You!

2

Randall stood in the doorway of the bedroom, trying to decide why he felt uneasy. Kolvek stood bulkily behind him; his presence was not intimidating, but it could not be ignored.

Randall had been in the Kolvek house for half an hour; he had already been shown through the rooms on the ground floor. It seemed to him that there was something schizophrenic about the house. The living room had rigidly structured conversational groupings; the sofas were rather stiff with scroll backs; there were careful little collections of porcelain knick-knacks, and bland landscapes on the walls which were dully beige like the wall-to-wall carpet. The study contained nothing but a bare desk, a swivel chair, a file cabinet and a straight chair. No curtains, just shades on the windows. The inhabitants of the house seemed to have differing tastes.

In the kitchen were a blender, a Cuisinart,

a capuccino maker, a pasta machine and a myriad of other gadgets whose purpose he didn't know. They were spotlessly clean, and looked as though they had never been used. The same was true of the copper pots hanging above the stove and the neat row of knives in their heavy wooden holder. The only thing out of place was a battered coffee maker — an old model, without digital readouts, timers or anything else. Its sole purpose was to make coffee and it looked as though it were used often. A bag of coffee, a measuring spoon and some filters stood on the counter next to it.

And now the master bedroom. End tables flanking a king-sized bed; lamps on both, an alarm clock and a phone on one. Nothing else. Not even a book to break up the neat surfaces.

Heavy rust velvet draperies matched the bedspread, and harmonized with the deep brown carpeting. The room really did not fit with the rooms downstairs. The lack of clutter reminded him of Kolvek's study, but the subtle blending of colors and fabrics was far removed from the self-conscious fussiness of the living room. In other words, nothing in the room seemed to belong to Sharon Kolvek.

The walk-in closet held only a few suits and shirts, with folded underthings and sweaters on some shelves and boots and shoes lined up on wire racks. All male.

The other bedrooms had looked like

unused guest rooms; maybe that was misleading. He turned to Kolvek.

"Where's your wife's room?"

Kolvek looked at him. "This was our room."

"She didn't have a separate bedroom?"

Kolvek stared at him for a little longer. "We were married," he said flatly. That seemed to be that. Obviously Kolvek believed that husband and wife had a duty to share one bedroom, no matter what happened to the relationship.

"Well, but then where are your wife's things? You know, her clothes, her shoes, her ... cosmetics ..."

"Oh, those." His face was inscrutable. "I got rid of them."

"You stored them?"

"No. I gave them to a thrift shop. I didn't have any use for them."

Randall had a sinking feeling. But he kept his fingers mentally crossed as he asked the next question. "How long after she left did you do that? Long enough so you thought she wasn't coming back?"

Kolvek looked surprised. It was the only real emotion he had shown all day. "No, I think it was two or three days later. What was the use of keeping them?"

Randall closed his eyes for a moment. It was not going to be a point in their favor if it got out that Kolvek had disposed of all his wife's belongings a couple of days after her disappearance. Of course you could always argue that he had done it in a fit of rage and grief — a desire to eliminate all traces of a disloyal wife. But Kolvek's impassive exterior might make that hard to imagine. And anyway it would be a mistake to plant the idea that Kolvek had an ungovernable temper.

On the other hand, probably Kolvek had just coldly decided that if his wife had chosen not to live with him any more, he did not need her possessions cluttering up his space. He was obviously a man who always cut his losses quickly and cleanly. What was done was done and it would be handled somehow.

He moved briskly on. "Okay then, I guess we're done up here. Why don't we go on down and get those charge bills now? And if you have any personal papers — diaries, that kind of thing — that you don't want people poking through, you'd better give them to me too. They can always get a search warrant."

Kolvek shook his head. "I don't have anything like that."

As they walked down the stairs, Randall slid his hand admiringly over the sleek bannister. "This looks like a really well-built house. Is it your work?"

Kolvek shook his head again. "No. I bought this house just after it was finished. The contractor was a fellow named Reese; he does good work. All I did was change the fireplace in the living room. And I did some work on the grounds."

Randall was struck suddenly by a thought; he should have thought of it earlier. Maybe the decorating hadn't been done by Sharon Kolvek at all. "Did the contractor do the interior decorating? Or did you hire someone?"

Kolvek began to shake his head again. "No. Sharon did it all." Naturally. Kolvek wouldn't even think of hiring a decorator. It was part of a wife's job to make a home for her husband.

"Did you bring much furniture from your old house?"

"No, nothing. It was time to move on."

Randall felt a first faint stirring of sympathy for the unknown Sharon Kolvek. It struck him that she was not really suited to live in this community, and he thought she might have liked to bring some of her favorite familiar things with her.

In the study Randall was riffling through the charge bills when the doorbell rang. He was expecting Bud Janis, the D.A.'s investigator, so he followed Kolvek out into the entry hall. But the young man who stood there, wearing soiled khaki pants and a petulant expression, was obviously not from the D.A.'s office. He handed Kolvek a packet of papers.

"This is my son Thomas, Mr Randall," Kolvek said. He began to look through the papers. Thomas stood there uneasily for a few minutes. Randall noticed that he had apparently been the victim of a particularly savage bout of adolescent acne.

"Is there any further word?" Thomas asked Kolvek.

"If you mean about the body that was found, no. It isn't definite yet that it's your mother. I told you yesterday that I thought it might be, and I don't know any more about it today." Randall wondered why he was so curt with his son. Certainly it was understandable that the boy would be anxious to know whether his mother was dead.

"Well," Thomas said, "okay." He was obviously going to leave. Randall decided he might as well use this opportunity to get some more background.

"If you have a minute, Mr Kolvek? I'd like to talk to you."

Thomas Kolvek shot a nervous glance at his father's granite face. There was obviously not going to be any help there.

"Okay," he said. "Sure."

They went into the living room and Randall chose what he thought looked like the least uncomfortable chair in the grouping near the fireplace. As soon as he sat down, he realized he had made a mistake. For whatever purpose this chair had been designed, it was not to accommodate the human body. The back pinched him between the shoulder blades and the springs jabbed at his buttocks. He leaned forward and took a legal pad out of his briefcase. Thomas was sitting opposite him on the sofa; Kolvek stood in front of the fireplace.

"Thomas—I hope you don't mind if I call you Thomas? I think otherwise we'll have too many Mr Kolveks in this room."

It was certainly a small joke, designed to ease the noticeable tension a little. But it misfired.

"I don't mind if you call me Thomas, but we all know there's only one Mr Kolvek in this room."

After Thomas delivered this little jab, he turned suddenly red, as if he just realized what he had said. He darted a look at his father and nervously smoothed his straggly mustache. He seemed to be overreacting. Kolvek stared calmly out the window.

"Well, anyway Thomas, let's go back to the Tuesday night dinner in August. Why don't you tell me what you remember about that?"

"There isn't anything to tell. We had dinner here, that's all, one big happy family. Halfway through dinner an argument started —I don't even remember what it was about. Then after dinner Susan had to leave to put her kids to bed and Elaine started acting up; she pulled Don away from the whiskey bottle and they left right after Susan did."

"Don is your sister Elaine's husband?"

"That's right, Don the great stockbroker. Maybe he gets his information from the whiskey dregs... you know, like tea leaves."

Kolvek interjected from the fireplace. "I don't know what you've been drinking, but my whiskey doesn't have any dregs." He did not look at his son.

Thomas flushed again. Randall tried to bring him back on track.

"So you were here with your parents after they all left. Was anybody else here?"

"No."

"No maid? Housekeeper?"

Joseph Kolvek answered that one. "Marie only comes in for a couple of hours in the morning during the week. She was long gone that night."

"So there were just the three of you. What happened next, Thomas?"

"Well, I didn't stay long. I wanted to talk to my parents about—something personal, but they weren't in a mood to listen, so I left."

Kolvek chose to clarify his son's answer again. "Thomas got caught in the middle of an argument we were having; he was too clumsy to keep out of the way. As usual. He irritated Sharon, she turned her big guns on him and he ran off with his tail between his legs. Also as usual."

"What do you mean by big guns?" Randall asked.

"Well, I'm not sure. It wasn't my fight; I

was just an observer. I guess they knew what they meant by all that talk about Thomas being his father's son and what-not. I don't."

"Thomas works for you?"

"Well, he's employed by me."

Thomas flushed again with anger. "All of this hasn't got anything to do with anything. When I left, my mother and father were still arguing and a couple days later Elaine called me to say she couldn't reach Ma. I told her I didn't know anything about it, and the next thing I know she's dragging me down here to talk to the police with her. I can't tell you anything else."

Randall wondered whether he really meant "can't" or "won't." But Thomas was on edge and it would be better not to push him. Janis was expected any moment; it wouldn't be a good time for Thomas to break down and start spilling out his resentments and all kinds of information about family skeletons. And sure enough, the doorbell rang. Kolvek started away from the fireplace, but Randall got up quickly and gestured to him to stay put. This was Kolvek's turf, but Randall wanted to leave no doubt in Janis's mind about who was in charge of the interview.

This time it was indeed Janis at the door. Randall shook hands with the tall, thin investigator and made some friendly chatter, wondering about the quickest, easiest way to get rid of Thomas Kolvek. It was one thing to have all these family hostilities out in the open with just the defense counsel there; it was another to risk Thomas going on some kind of official record in his present mood. He feared, though, that he was trying to lock the barn doors a little late.

Thomas was standing up, ready to leave, when they returned to the living room. Janis nodded at him amiably and said hello.

"You two know each other?" Randall asked.

"Yes," Janis said. "I talked to Mr Kolvek yesterday afternoon."

Randall gazed thoughtfully at Thomas's receding back as the young man walked rapidly to the hall. "Learn anything interesting?" he asked, casually.

Janis grinned. "Come on, Jim. No charges have been filed against anybody yet; certainly not against your client. And unless and until they are, I don't have to tell you a thing. And even if I did, you'd have to go through channels. And you know it."

Randall raised his hand in mock-defense. "Hey, okay, okay. It was just a shot. But I would like to know if you can tell me why the D.A.'s office is investigating an as-yet-to-be-identified body that may have died from natural causes."

"Sorry, Jim. I just do what I'm told to do. Why don't you ask the higher-ups about that? I'm just a flunky."

"And I'm just Winnie the Pooh," Randall

said. Janis was one of the D.A.'s best investigators. This investigation was not only premature: it was too heavy duty. Something was definitely up. But there wasn't much chance of finding anything out at the moment.

"Oh, sorry, Bud, I'd like you to meet my client, Joseph Kolvek. Mr Kolvek, Bud Janis works for the District Attorney's office." Randall had purposely avoided introducing Kolvek to see how swiftly and directly Janis would target in on him, but Janis was playing it cool, leaving it to Randall to set the pace. Possibly he knew a lot and could afford to bide his time, or maybe he didn't know anything at all and was just fishing, hoping to catch something. It was hard to tell.

"Why don't you have a seat, Bud?" he said pleasantly. "And could you give me your card for my file?"

"Sure." Janis handed over the card and settled down in what Randall now thought of as the Spanish Inquisition chair. He was obviously less adaptable than Randall, or perhaps less polite, because he got up again almost immediately and moved to the sofa. Randall laughed.

"I tried that chair too," he said. "But *I* stuck it out. I guess I've got more perseverance than you." He put up his big palm. "Wait. Don't say it, I know what you're thinking." He turned to Kolvek, who was staring at them. "Mr Janis is politely refraining from saying that what I've got is more padding, not more perseverance."

"Now would I say an insulting thing like that?" Janis asked. Throughout the banter and the laughter Kolvek remained unsmiling. Randall could not restrain a small sigh. He picked up his notepad and pen. There seemed to be no way to get Kolvek to relax and put people at ease.

Janis pulled out his own notebook. "All right, Mr Kolvek. I've read the missing persons report. Now why don't you tell me about it one more time, in your own words."

Kolvek recited the facts in his flat monotone. "We had a family dinner on the night of Tuesday, August sixth. We did that about once a month. My two daughters and their families left around eight-fifteen, eight-thirty. My son left about fifteen minutes later."

"Right, I've got that. Why don't you tell me, step by step, what you and Mrs Kolvek did when you were alone."

"I dumped a couple ashtrays because I don't like the smell of stale cigarettes. Other than that things were pretty much left for the maid in the morning. I went into the study to get some work done. My wife went upstairs, I think I remember hearing the shower run. A while later I heard her come back downstairs and the front door closed. I heard her car start up and drive off. She wasn't back yet when I went to bed about twelve-thirty."

Randall kept his face impassive. Inwardly he was raging at himself. It wasn't Kolvek's fault, it was his own fault that this was the first he had heard about Mrs Kolvek leaving the house that evening. There was no question in his mind that Kolvek was not trying to hide anything; he himself had just not asked the right questions. He had just assumed that Sharon Kolvek had stayed home Tuesday night. It crossed his mind to postpone the rest of this interview until he could get a better grip on things. But that would probably just give Janis ideas. On the surface it didn't look as though this development would do Kolvek any harm. It was just his paranoia about the unexpected that was upsetting him.

Kolvek went on. "The next day when I got home from work I checked the garage and her car wasn't there. Some clothes were gone too. I haven't heard from her since."

"What sort of car did your wife drive? Was it her car?"

"She drove a 1981 Chevette. We own it jointly, but she used it every day."

"What color was the car, Mr Kolvek?"

"Gray."

"And do you know the license number?"

"1-S-H-A-R-O-N."

"Sharon being your wife's first name, right? Okay, Mr Kolvek. Did you know where she might have gone?"

"She might have gone a number of

places. I don't know where she did go."

"Did you check around at all with relatives, friends...?"

"I believed that my wife had left me," Kolvek said calmly. "I certainly wasn't going to make a fool of myself running around trying to find her."

Janis asked, "Did your wife come home at all that Tuesday night or early Wednesday morning?"

"I don't know."

"You don't know? Did you have separate rooms?"

Kolvek did not have to answer questions of that sort, but Randall let it go. This was safe ground, at least for the moment.

"No, we did not. We shared the bedroom. But sometimes Sharon would take off for the evening. If she came in late she would sleep in one of the spare bedrooms. For all I know that's what she did that night."

"But didn't you notice whether or not her car was there in the morning?"

Kolvek shook his head. "My car was in the shop, so I didn't go into the garage. I took a cab to work."

Randall interrupted. "Why all these questions about the car, Bud?"

Janis apparently decided he wouldn't let out any secrets by answering that question. "We've found an abandoned vehicle not too far from where we found the body. It's in pretty bad shape—no license or I.D.

number... We're trying to trace it." He turned back to Kolvek. "And when you got home from work that Wednesday night, she was gone?"

"Yes."

"You have no idea whether she came home that night?"

"When I talked to Marie... that's the maid... When I asked Marie about it a couple of days later, she said Mrs Kolvek was not home when she got here Wednesday morning about nine-thirty. But my wife could have gone out again. I left for the yard about seven-thirty."

"Did you ask Marie if she'd seen your wife at all that day?"

"Yes. She hadn't seen her. But she leaves for the day about twelve-thirty, so even if Sharon did not come home Tuesday night, she could have come back Wednesday afternoon to get her clothes, and no one would have seen her. She came back and got them some time."

"Well," Janis said, "somebody got them some time."

There was a pause.

Janis looked at his notes for a moment and then asked again, "Where do you think your wife went that night, Mr Kolvek?"

Randall decided that Janis had had all the rope he was going to get. "Come on, Bud," he said, easily, "my client's given you all the facts he knows. He's told you he doesn't know where she went. His speculations or conjectures aren't your business."

"All I'm asking for is a little guidance about what direction we should be looking in. That's not unreasonable, Jim."

"Unreasonable is in the eye of the beholder. And my eye says that question is out of line." Ordinarily Randall would have let Kolvek answer that question, but these circumstances were not ordinary. He didn't want Kolvek responding to any more questions until he knew the answers himself. He hoped that Janis would mark his action down to an arbitrary exercise of authority rather than to a reflection of ignorance, which was what it was.

Janis accepted the limitation, for whatever reason, and moved on.

"Mr Kolvek, you told the Sheriff's office that you just assumed your wife had left you, is that right?"

Kolvek nodded. "Yes."

"You've had no indication about what happened to her after that?"

Randall spoke up again. "Mr Kolvek has not been contacted by Mrs Kolvek since that night."

The clock on the mantelpiece chimed softly. Janis glanced at it and closed his notebook. "I didn't realize it was getting so late." He stood up. "I want to thank both of you for your time, and if I need any more information from Mr Kolvek I'll be in touch with you, Jim."

Randall rose too, rather startled by this sudden move for departure.

"What's the hurry, Bud? We've answered your questions..." Janis looked at him quizzically and he grimaced. "All right, we've answered most of your questions. Now how about answering a few of ours? Just what is going on in this case?"

"Oh, come on, Jim. All I can tell you is that we have a body which we have reason to believe is Mrs Kolvek's, and we're doing a little preliminary work."

"Preliminary hell! Try premature. We're not even sure that it is Mrs Kolvek — and if it is, we don't know that she didn't die from natural causes."

"Well, you know that every unusual death has to be investigated. This is just routine."

"But *you're* not routine, Bud," Randall said.

Janis smiled. "I told you before, I just do what I'm told. And right now I've been told to go someplace else. So if Mr Kolvek doesn't want to add anything to his statement..." Kolvek looked stolidly back at him. "... then I'll take off." He shook hands with Kolvek, and again with Randall in the entryway. "Thanks again for setting this up so soon, Jim. Like I said, I'll be in touch."

Randall stood in the doorway, staring thoughtfully after Janis's car.

"Something bothering you?" Kolvek asked.

Randall closed the door slowly. "It's too much, too soon," he said, almost to himself. "And where's he going in such a hurry? You'd have thought he'd press a little more. He didn't even ask anything about the argument at the dinner table." He leaned against the wall. "Okay. Do you have any questions about what's going on?"

"Just one. Why didn't you tell him about the credit cards, about the bills? That's important, isn't it? It shows she was still alive."

"Well, I always like to hold these things until they can have maximum impact," Randall said. "Before I forget, there's one thing I need to check. Is a full-scale investigation going to turn up any history of domestic violence?"

Kolvek looked blank.

"I mean, if the neighbors are asked about it, are they going to say that you beat your wife? If he searches the records, is Janis going to find out that the police had to come in here to mediate an argument?"

Kolvek looked him in the eye. "I don't know what the neighbors might say," he said. "And there is one police report, about seven years ago. My wife threw an iron at me, and I hit her. The lady next door called the police because she was a born-again Christian and she didn't like Sharon's language. Sharon was screaming at me at the top of her lungs."

Randall decided to let it go at that. He would learn what the neighbors thought soon enough, and Jenny could get the police report for him. "All right. About your wife leaving that night — where *do* you think she went?"

"She could have gone any number of places. I don't know where she went."

Kolvek was so buttoned up he couldn't relax even when it would help him to do it. Randall sighed. "Mr Kolvek, I'm your attorney. Nothing you say to me is going to be used against you. All I want to know is what you think. Do you know where she usually went?"

Kolvek stared at him for a minute. He was weighing the situation. He seemed to be a man who weighed every situation. "She usually went to the Sunset Bar to start," he said, "and then she went on from there."

Randall tried to cover up his surprise. The Sunset Bar was not exactly a dive, but it wasn't a friendly neighborhood watering hole, either. It attracted serious drinkers and swingers and its reputation was not great. He would not have connected the woman who lived in this bland, conventional house with a place like that.

He cut off the conversation, and said goodbye to Kolvek. He got into his car, thinking about Jenny. He hoped Sally had been able to get hold of her. It looked as though this case was going to need a talented investigator.

JAMES R. RANDALL

Attorney at Law
616 South Sherman Boulevard, Suite 2102
Racine, California
611/445-3123

September 16, 1985

BANKCARD SERVICES
1000 South Morega
Richardson, California

>   RE: Account Number 0300-4252-91250
>   Cardholders: Joseph and Sharon Kolvek

Dear Bankcard Services:

Enclosed you will find an authorization to release information concerning the above-referenced account.

Please forward to me copies of all charge slips received by you in connection with said account for the period August 6 to September 10 of this year. In that connection I am providing herewith a check in an amount not to exceed $50.00 for your costs in processing this request.

Time is of importance in this matter, and I would accordingly appreciate your giving this request your expedited attention. Thank you for your courtesy and cooperation.

Very truly yours,

James R Randall

James R. Randall

JRR/sc
Enclosure

3

Randall knew something was up as soon as he walked through his office door after his morning's appearance in court. Sally and Jenny, the investigator, were in the reception area, looking very pleased with themselves. Sally opened her mouth when she saw him, but he cut her off.

"Whatever it is, it's going to have to wait. We've got to do something on Roberts first."

"Something go wrong in court?"

"That's one of the great understatements of all time. The jerk 'forgot' to tell me he had a felony conviction in Nebraska under an alias. The information didn't come through in time for the probation report, but it came in time for today's sentence hearing. And it shot my entire presentation right out of the water—I was pushing that everyone's entitled to one mistake."

"But you can't let Roberts go to jail,"

Sally said. "His wife and kids would be on welfare in a week!"

"I know that," Randall said impatiently. "Fortunately, the Nebraska prior came up before I started my spiel, so I was able to ask for a continuance. We've got two weeks to try and repair the damage. Right now we have to find somebody in a place called York, Nebraska, to send us the court records on the old case so I can find out just what it is we're facing. You check the Martindale-Hubbell directories while I get my notes together."

He picked up his briefcase from Sally's desk and strode into his office, closing the door behind him. A second later he poked his head out again.

"Hello, Jenny," he said. "Can you hang on a few minutes? We won't be long."

"My time is your time."

Half an hour later, the three of them sat in Randall's office. The emergency was under control. Randall leaned back in his chair and put his feet up on the desk.

"Okay. Now tell me what you were looking so pleased about when I came in."

There was a short pause. Sally and Jenny exchanged glances.

"Well, actually," Sally said, "the news is bad. We were just sort of pleased that we were able to get it. It's about the Kolvek case. I called the coroner's office to find out when the autopsy would be scheduled. They've had the body about a week now. That's really only four working days, so given that backup over there I figured it would be another couple of weeks. But — they said it was scheduled for this afternoon."

Randall's feet came off the desk onto the floor with a crash. He looked at her in astonishment. "What the hell!"

"My reaction exactly. I tried to feel around a little bit but I had to keep it low profile. So all I found out was that the Deputy District Attorney handling this case is Elizabeth Barron."

Randall whistled softly. "Hot stuff."

The phone rang in the outer office and Sally went to answer it.

"Elizabeth Barron is definitely hot stuff," Randall said to Jenny. "She's got a knack, a real knack." It was a knack for press manipulation.

Elizabeth Barron had entered the District Attorney's office five years earlier, obviously intending to be its first female District Attorney, no mean feat in this conservative county. Since she would need to get elected, she went out for name recognition. She easily circumvented the rule that all press releases had to come from the liaison division by just happening to be there whenever the cameras started rolling. And she couldn't just say "no comment," could she? It wouldn't be good public relations. Consequently most of her colleagues weren't crazy about her, but Jim Collins, chief of the D.A.'s criminal division gave her a free rein and sat back to watch the fireworks. He wasn't worried about his job as long as the present D.A. was in office, and the community never went out of its way to get rid of a D.A. In the meantime Barron was good for the D.A.'s image. She was dedicated, intelligent, aggressive and she got results. And because she was so quotable the results got headlines. When she fell on her face once in a while the D.A.'s people just shook their heads indulgently and refused to accept responsibility.

Randall respected her as a lawyer. But when he went to law school there hadn't been any courses on speaking to reporters. So when he was asked questions he was inclined to give background as well as current status. That gave the press a better understanding of the case, but when they chopped up his replies to fit the space they had, he usually didn't sound very impressive. Barron, on the other hand, had a knack for the colorful phrase. There were lots of times when the phrase was too colorful. There was the time, for instance, when she called one of his clients who had set off some firecrackers in a shopping mall "an incendiary revolutionary." That made a nice headline in the afternoon paper, and it also put a lot of pressure on the judge to commit to prison rather than to impose probation. And the client in question was really just a dope; he wasn't malicious, as Barron knew perfectly well.

Randall hoped he had learned a lesson from his encounters with her. Naturally he thought over all the clever things *he* could have said, and he came up with one, after the fact, of course: "Mrs Barron's elephant gun is once again pointed at a mouse." Maybe he could still use it sometime. As it was, his response had been cut in the newspaper reports and he sounded evasive, which made things worse for his client. After three years of law school and twenty years of law practice all his instincts told him to elaborate succinctly, but now he was almost looking forward to adapting to the public spotlight and giving Barron a run for her money. The last time they had met in court it had been a draw.

Sally came back into the office. She was smiling. "That was Doug Jeffreys — you know, the kid who was caught with the kilo of marijuana? Well, he was thinking about his case over the weekend and he decided the best thing he could do is move to another state. So he wants you to tell the D.A. that he's moving to Florida so the charges against him can be dismissed because he won't be living here any more."

After a pause Randall said carefully, "Are you telling me that he thinks he can just move out of the state and the prosecutor will drop the charges?"

"That seems to be the idea. I told him things didn't exactly work that way."

After the three of them stopped laughing, Randall said, "Well, you've got to admit, this job would be pretty boring if it weren't for the clients."

"It wouldn't be too profitable either," Sally said drily. "Listen, about this Elizabeth Barron thing. Why would she jump on the bandwagon this early? I thought we didn't even know if there was a case yet. So I asked Jenny to look into it for us."

"And?" Randall looked at Jenny expectantly. She seemed about sixteen years old, with short, curly red-gold hair, freckles spattered across a pug nose, and a slight build. But in her case appearances were certainly deceptive. She had been with the police department for six years, and had left because it frustrated her to be distracted when she was working on a case. She didn't like heavy caseloads and lots of paper work. But she was also very careful to take plenty of direction from Randall, and he liked that because he was leery of investigators who relied basically on their own initiative. Sometimes they turned up matters which would have been better left buried. And Jenny went out of her way to avoid confrontations. She used her innocent appearance to disarm people. She was never pushy or offensive and she knew instinctively when to back off.

"Well," she said, "the bottom line is that Elaine Morris—you know, the daughter—is apparently really pushing this. Her husband's family has political connections. So A went to B who talked to C who talked to the D.A. Like that. So this case is going to get a lot of careful attention."

"Damn," Randall said softly.

"Can't prove anything," Jenny said. "But that's the way it went."

Randall stared out the window at the harbor without seeing it. That explained the premature investigation, the heavy-weight attention. They couldn't railroad Kolvek, of course; after all, he had his own connections through his ties to the contractors association. But they weren't going to give him the benefit of any doubts either. Now it would be necessary to take an offensive posture; reacting defensively wouldn't work.

"One other thing we found out," Sally said. He came out of his trance and looked at her. "Somebody hustled the dental records out to the coroner's office over the weekend. And it's Sharon Kolvek, all right. Or it was."

Randall nodded. He had already assumed that the body was his client's wife. So that loose end was tied up. And now he knew where Bud Janis was hurrying to last Saturday morning.

"Okay," he said. "The first thing to do is get someone to monitor this autopsy. I'd like a pathologist, but if we have to we can make do with a forensic biologist. Sally, get Dave Briggs on the phone at the university's department of medicine, will you? Then call the coroner's office and find out exactly what time the autopsy is scheduled for; tell them we represent the husband of the deceased and we will have an observer there. In fact, you better call the coroner's office first. Okay?"

"You don't think the coroner's office is going to try and pull anything, do you?" Sally asked.

"No, not really." He shook his head. "They work closely with the D.A.'s office, but they're pretty independent over there. But I think in this case we're going to need any edge we can get. If there's the slightest question about anything, I want someone knowledgeable there watching out for our interests."

Sally went off and Randall turned to Jenny.

"I think we can assume that the D.A.'s investigation is going to move along pretty fast. So I want everything you get as soon as you get it. Don't kill yourself or anything but I want you to be aware of that. I know you've got the basics, but remember that as things stand right now it's going to be hard to prove our client is innocent. Apart from anything else, it would be a hell of a job establishing the exact date of death after all this time, so an alibi defense is out."

Jenny smiled. "Whatever happened to innocent until proven guilty?"

Randall snorted. "You know as well as I do that in an investigation — as opposed to a trial—things are reversed. They seem to decide who's guilty and then look for the evidence to prove it. And naturally any time a wife is murdered, the husband's the prime suspect. Especially when there's been domestic violence."

"Domestic violence? Sally didn't tell me that."

"Oh, Lord, right, thanks for reminding me. About seven years ago the cops were called in on a domestic quarrel at the Kolvek's. This was before they moved out here. They lived in the city, so it was the police department, not the sheriff's office. I want you to track down the reports on that and get me a copy; I'll give you an authorization.

"Anyway, to get back to the point—we can't really prove he didn't do it, so we're going to have to show that several other people could have done it. We want them to understand that if they charge Kolvek there's so much mud around they'll never get over the reasonable doubt standard. And from what I've heard about Sharon Kolvek, we won't have any trouble finding the mud. It would be nice if we could find out who actually did it, while we're nosing around, but it isn't strictly necessary for us.

"Now over the weekend I found out that Sharon Kolvek left the house on Tuesday, August sixth, and first of all we want to know where she went. Our client says she sometimes went to the Sunset Bar, so that's where you have to start. I'll give you a photo..."

The intercom buzzed and he picked it up. Sally had Dr Briggs on the line.

Randall pushed the button. "Dave! How's it going?"

"As usual, Jim, just as usual. What do you need from me this time?"

"Now, Dave," Randall drawled. "That really hurts. Why should you think just because I called I want something?"

Briggs made a rude noise. "Because I've known you for fifteen years, that's why. Cut the bull. What's up?"

"Well, now that you mention it, I do need something—"

"—I knew it—"

"—I need a pathologist to watch an autopsy at the coroner's office..."

"When?"

"This afternoon." Quickly Randall held the receiver away from his ear to deaden the roar he knew was coming. He was not disappointed.

"Christ, Jim! Can't you ever do anything on a normal time schedule? I'm beginning to think all law schools require advanced courses in procrastination."

A few choice experiences he had had in doctor's offices flitted through Randall's mind, but he decided against bringing them up. "Dave, it wasn't my fault this time. Honest, I just found out about it half an hour ago.

So have you got anybody with a free afternoon who would like to earn a little extra money?"

"How am I supposed to know something like that? The doctors in this department don't have to clear their schedules with me. Okay, I'll check for you. I do know one really bright young man who's a dynamite pathologist. He might be interested."

"Hold it, Dave," Randall said. "I don't want to be a pain, but what do you mean, 'young'?"

Briggs sighed. "I know you don't want to be a pain, Jim, it just comes to you naturally. When I say 'young', I mean just out of residency."

"That's what I was afraid you meant. Now Dave, listen, I need somebody who's qualified in court before. If worst comes to worst and I have to use independent testimony on the autopsy, I can't have the D.A. knocking it down by questioning the guy's credentials before he even starts."

"The only way he can qualify in court is to testify in court. And according to you he can't testify until he qualifies. Is this logical?"

Randall sighed. They had gone over this before. "Listen, Dave, there are attorneys who would take the chance. The legal profession hasn't cornered the market on Catch-22s, we both know that. But I can't afford to give your protege's career a boost when I'm playing with my client's future. Now come on, Dave . . ."

"Okay, okay, I'll find someone a hundred years old. I'll get back to you. Yes, right away, right away."

"I really appreciate it." Randall hung up, smiling. Briggs was a true iconoclast. He tilted at every windmill he saw. Randall was selective about his windmills; he saw too many to pick up his lance each time. He buzzed Sally and told her Briggs would be calling back.

"Sorry, Jenny. Where were we?"

"The picture. Sharon Kolvek's picture."

"Oh, right." He dug it out and handed it to her. "It's relatively new. Not more than six months or so old."

Jenny looked at the snapshot carefully. A woman standing on a lawn in the sun. In her mid-fifties or so with bouffant brown hair, wearing a dark blue dress and high heels. And gloves. Jenny couldn't remember the last time she had seen a woman wearing white gloves in the afternoon in Southern California.

She put the photo in her handbag. "Okay, you want me to start at the Sunset Bar, find out if she was there on Tuesday, August sixth, and if she wasn't, whether anybody there knows where she might have gone. Right. Now can you tell me about anybody else who might give me something to go on? Her husband, maybe? Family? Friends? Or don't you want me to contact any of them?"

Randall frowned. "Well, of course you can call the client, Kolvek, if you want to. I've told him you'll be working for me so he'll know who you are." he smiled suddenly. "You ought to get along great with him. You've got a lot in common—both the strong, silent type."

Jenny laughed. But he thought about it a moment. Jenny and Kolvek were both similar on the surface—both silent, controlled, observant. But Jenny's silence seduced people into confiding in her; sometimes they almost forgot she was there and seemed to be talking to themselves. But Kolvek's silence was dominating, overbearing. With Jenny silence was an instrument for self-effacement; with Kolvek it was a weapon for control.

"I don't think you'll get much from Kolvek," he said. "He doesn't seem to know or care where his wife went. But, as I say, you can talk to him. Just remember the fine line we're walking whenever you talk directly to the client."

"I know," Jenny said. There was a fine but important legal distinction between reports from an investigator working for an attorney who represented a client and reports from an investigator working directly for the client. One was discoverable, the other was not. The law in California was currently staggering drunkenly all over that fine line of distinction, but Jenny was always very careful to follow Randall's instructions exactly.

Everything done by her must be kept within the attorney/client or work product privileges.

"How about family, friends?"

"We're going to have to be careful about that. There are a lot of family stresses in this case, so I don't want you interviewing any of them unless I'm there too. I'm sorry, I know that hamstrings you. What I'm doing is asking you to conduct an investigation without talking to anyone. But if you get a line on particular friends, you can follow that up. Just stay in touch with me. And when you ask around Kolvek's neighborhood be more careful than usual. We want to keep this as low-key as we can. He has a lot to lose, and I don't mean just if charges are filed. I understand he's a mover with the contractors association and he could become vice-president of the national association. They don't need any more scandals, so we want to keep a lid on publicity as much as we can."

Jenny wrote for a while in her notebook. She looked up. "Anything else?"

"I'm going to need a rundown on the family. Check out the places where they've lived, find out what the neighbors think of them. I know that's tough when you can't talk to the family themselves, but go back as far as you can. Try to give me a feel for the family, and I'd like a clear picture of what Mrs Kolvek was like. You'll need some extra help with this part of it and I'll leave all the details of that up to you. I guess that's about it."

"Right." She shoved the notebook into her bag and they both rose. Randall showed her out of the office and as the door closed behind her, Sally said, "Okay, we've got a Dr Jordan Emery lined up for the autopsy, which is going to be at two. Dr Briggs told me to tell you that Dr Emery is good for an hour's boredom in court." She looked inquiring.

"Oh, just a little joke. You know how dull it is, going over expert's credentials. Dave's just telling us that Emery has a lot of credentials."

"I've got the charge company letters ready," Sally said. Obviously she didn't see anything funny about credentials. While he skimmed the letters rapidly, and signed them, Sally asked, "Are you going to sit in on the autopsy?"

Randall grimaced. "I guess so. It's not my favorite thing, but I'm sure Bud Janis is going to be there. And Elizabeth might just decide to show up, too. A little show of strength on our part won't hurt. You'd better call Sam Josephs and tell him I won't be able to have lunch with him. I've got a strong stomach, but there's no sense tempting fate. Well, now I better get some work done for somebody besides Kolvek."

He picked up some message slips from the desk, and went back into his office to get on with the day's work.

TOXICOLOGY REPORT

OFFICE OF THE CORONER
County of San Marin

File Number:	07124E49
NAME:	KOLVEK, Sharon Susan
SPECIMEN SUBMITTED:	Bowel Contents, Liver, Kidney
ANALYSIS REQUESTED:	Homicide screen
SPECIMEN SUBMITTED BY:	Cecilia Mayrick, M.D. Examining Room

REPORT

9/17/85

Liver:
- Barbiturates — Not Detected
- Halogenated Hydrocarbons — Not Detected
- Ethyl Alcohol — Present
- Ethchlorvynol — Not Detected
- Basic Fraction — Negative
- Salicylic Acid — Not Detected
- Carbamates, glutethimide, methyprylon, methaqualone — Not Detected

Morphine:
- Lung — Not Detected
- Bile — Not Detected

JAMES R. BREAN
Chief Toxicologist

4

Jenny parked and got out of her Honda Accord. The parking lot of the Sunset Bar was quiet in the early afternoon; there were only three cars in the cramped spaces, including her own.

She walked up to the long, low building. Cedar bark covered the ground around the walkway, with a few bushes planted here and there. She took hold of the beaten metal handle on one of the carved massive wooden double doors and passed through into the shadowy interior, stumbling for a moment on two dimly-lit steps. The bar ran the considerable length of the room; small tables were scattered about, none with more than two chairs.

The bartender was a wiry man in his mid-twenties, wearing jeans and a short-sleeved gray sweatshirt.

"Something I can help you with, honey?"

She knew he thought she was a schoolgirl looking for a telephone or some change for the bus. "Sure," she said. She climbed up onto one of the red-leather barstools. "I'll take a beer, please."

"Let's see an I.D.," he said stonily. When she gave him her drivers license, he checked the picture against her face twice, taking his time about it. "Okay," he said reluctantly. He handed back the license. "Sorry. We get enough hassles here; we don't need any more. So what kind of beer you want? Lite, Coors, Michelob..."

"A medium glass of Bass?"

He looked a little surprised. "Okay. One Bass for the lady."

After he gave her the beer and took her money, he indicated his willingness to chat by staying near her and making a few passes at the spotless bar before her with a wet cloth.

"I'm Jenny," she said.

"Hi. I'm Joe... So what brings you here?"

"Oh, I don't know. Isn't there some kind of rule that says that at some time or other everybody's got to come to the Sunset Bar?"

He grinned. "I never heard that, but it's all right with me. I own half the place."

A door behind the bar opened suddenly, revealing a man in his late thirties with a forehead creased with worry lines.

"Where'd you put the invoice for that last delivery from Sunny's?" he asked abruptly.

"Top of the filing cabinet," Joe said.

The man grunted. "It might help the bookkeeping a little if you'd put the invoices in the slot marked 'invoices'. I know that's a lot to ask, but just humor me, will you?"

He went back into his office and shut the door behind him.

Joe raised his eyebrows at Jenny. "Old Bob there. He sort of lets things get him down."

"He your accountant?"

He laughed. "Na, he's my partner. We've only had the place eighteen months."

"What's getting him down? From what I hear your business is booming."

Joe hesitated a moment, and then looked down the bar. With an apologetic smile he moved down toward the end to serve a customer who had just come in. When he came back he automatically took a few more swipes at the surface in front of her. "Well," he said, "this wasn't exactly what we had in mind when we started out. Bob wanted a nice family kind of bar. You know ... people stop by after a movie, shoppers come in, regulars watch the ball game on TV ... I mean, we're in walking distance of a couple movies, a theatre in the shopping mall. We even talked the city into giving us an extra street light so customers could feel safe walking over here at night. And look at those doors. A friend of Bob's built them. Bob wanted everybody to know right from the doors that the place has style."

He sighed and shook his head, idly continuing his attack on the formica. "So how could we know the switch-and-swap crowd would like the place? Overnight we got a reputation; this is the place for action."

He stared at the circles his hand was making on the bar. "Bob is the one who saved his money for this. I just kind of went along for the ride. He can't adjust." He smiled. "But while it lasts, we're really raking in the money. These people will pay double the price for half the drink." He looked suddenly a little disconcerted. "Jesus, I don't know why I'm dumping all this on you. You're one hell of a good listener, you know that? Why don't I give you one on the house to make up for all this talk?"

Jenny held up her glass, still half full. "Oh, thanks, I'm fine. I think it's awfully interesting, no kidding."

She hesitated. He looked at her shrewdly.

"Why do I get the feeling you didn't just drop in for a cold beer on a hot afternoon?"

She smiled at him, grateful that he had made it easy to bring up the subject on her mind. "You're pretty sharp," she said. "I'm enjoying the beer and the conversation. But actually I'm doing a little investigating — "

"No kidding! You're a private investigator? What're you doing, getting the goods on somebody's old lady?"

"Why, do you get a lot of that kind of thing here?"

"Nope, we've never gotten any. I been sort of expecting it, but no luck so far. I guess with the new divorce laws it doesn't matter so much any more."

"No, I guess not, except maybe in custody cases. But I'm not here for anything like that." She took Sharon Kolvek's picture out of her bag. "I just want to get some information on this woman."

She had decided, on Randall's advice, not to mention that Sharon was dead, on the theory that people might not cooperate if there was any question of homicide. Now she thought that Joe would probably enjoy the excitement, but she stayed with her original decision.

He looked closely at the picture. "I don't know..." he said doubtfully. Then suddenly his face cleared and he snapped his fingers. "Hey, yeah, I think I do know her. She's a regular. Or she was, anyway. I haven't seen her for quite a while. Hey, why don't I ask Bob?"

He opened the door to the office and called. "Bob, you want to come out here for a minute?"

Bob came one step out of his room. "What is it? I'm right in the middle of something."

"This is Jenny," Joe said pleasantly. "She wants to know what we can tell her about this lady here." Bob moved reluctantly to take the snapshot. Jenny was surprised to see his face change suddenly when he looked at it. He tossed it onto the bar and said with what seemed to be strained casualness, "Well, I don't know her name. I haven't seen her in here for a while, but she used to be a regular."

"How regular?" Jenny asked.

"Well. I'll bet it's five weeks since she came in the last time. Before that she was coming in a couple of evenings a week. She was kind of different."

"Different? How?"

He paused for a moment. "Sorry. I can't help you," he said stiffly.

He turned back to his doorway. "Hey," Joe said. "This little lady's just doing a job. She's okay . . . likes the beer."

Bob hesitated again. "All I can say is what I just said. She wasn't like the rest of them."

Joe stared at him for a minute and then snapped his fingers again. "Hey, you're right! I remember now. Whew." He shook his fingers as if they had been burnt. "Different is right."

Bob nodded at Jenny. "I'll be getting back then," he said, and returned to his office and closed the door.

"You want another beer?" She nodded, to be friendly. He talked while he went through the motions.

"You know, most people who come here fit into one or two categories. They come to make it with someone or they just want to get drunk. But her," he tapped the photo with his knuckle, "she didn't fit into either of those. What she wanted—"

He broke off to answer a summons from farther down the bar. Business was beginning to pick up as people finished work for the day. Time was running out. Knowing from experience that people's moods were subject to sudden changes, Jenny waited nervously for him to come back. When he did she was relieved that he picked up where he had left off.

"I was saying that she used to come in here once or twice a week, for about six months. She'd order a Bloody Mary and nurse it for maybe four or five hours, the whole time she was here. She was real friendly to the guys that came up to her, and you'd be surprised how many did that. She didn't look like she looks in this photo, at least not when she came in here she didn't. Everything about her said, 'Come get me, I'm worth your time.' The end of the evening she'd pick some guy and huddle with him for a while and then leave with him."

"Isn't that pretty much what women do in here?"

He nodded. "Oh sure. We thought so too. But after a while we'd notice some of the guys she left with coming back into the bar after just a couple minutes. Well, you know, sometimes that happens. Something doesn't work out, you know how it is. But these guys came back looking like they been hit in the gut and they were real touchy. A couple of them picked fights, it looked like just for the hell of it.

"Listen, one night I heard a guy talking about her to his buddies. He said lay off — " He broke off again to answer another call. Jenny was ready to scream with frustration.

He was gone longer this time. When he came back he asked her if she wanted another beer. She didn't but she said she did. He got it for her and then said abruptly, "Okay. I can't prove it and I sure wouldn't swear to it anywhere, but what this broad was, was a — " He paused and swallowed. "Well, she was a tease. She'd lead them on, and then drop them hard. And I guess she was pretty nasty about it. She let them know she was available, but they didn't qualify. Everybody she left with didn't come back in, but I'm willing to bet she never left the parking lot with any of them. She got her kicks out of putting them down and then she left."

He went off again to take another order and Jenny drank her beer, knowing that was about it for the afternoon. When he came back she spoke to him quickly, before he could tell her he was too busy for any more conversation.

"I really appreciate your taking the time to tell me all this. I'd just like to ask you a couple quick questions, if you don't mind. Could you give me the name of anybody she might come in here with, or maybe hang around with?" This was a stab in the dark; she didn't expect anything to come of it. To her surprise, he nodded.

"Yeah, you might try Brenda Simms. They hung around together. I think this Simms got a real boot out of your lady. She might be able to tell you something."

She flashed him a brilliant smile. This was something, a solid lead.

"Gee, I really appreciate this. Do you think Mrs Simms might be in here tonight?"

He shook his head. "Na, I doubt it. I haven't seen her in here for a little while. She's been kind of tailing off."

"You wouldn't happen to know where I could reach her, would you?"

She wasn't surprised when he shook his head again. As she slid off the barstool, she decided she might as well make a fool of herself with one last question.

"Just for the record, do you remember if the woman I'm asking about was in here on August sixth? A Tuesday?"

His good nature was wearing thin. "Come on," he said, "that was five, six weeks ago. I don't even remember who came in here last night. She stopped coming in a while ago, that's all I can tell you."

"Sure, you're right," she said. "But listen, I really appreciate your time..."

"Wait a minute," he said suddenly. "Hang on, I'll be right back."

He disappeared into the office. Jenny stood by the barstool, organizing her notepad and pencil into her bag. There was a second bartender on duty now, people scattered down the barside, a few tables with women. No couples yet, anyway. And not much conversation.

"Looks sort of innocent, doesn't it?" Joe was back. "But it isn't even five yet," he said. "They're just trying out their wings. The hard-core starts drifting in after seven. This is like a Cub Scout troop; later it'll be a Marine boot camp. Anyway, here's what I wanted to give you."

It was a card with Brenda Simms' name and address.

"She was one of the regulars before things changed here," he said. "We were running tabs for some customers, she was one of them. This address is more than a year old, so maybe it's wrong now. But anyway it's a start."

She copied the information carefully from the card and gave it back to him. He waved away her thanks and went off down the bar. She had helped to liven up a dull afternoon for him, but now he was getting down to business.

Outside, Jenny paused a moment as her eyes adjusted to the bright sunlight of a late September afternoon. Then she walked to her car. Shortly, she thought, the bar would be dropped as a pickup station and some other bar would become popular. These things happened very fast; it was hard to keep track of them. But in the last several months the Sunset had gained a very scummy reputation.

She pulled into a gas station with a pay phone. For a change Randall was in and available. She told him what she had learned from Joe and accepted his low whistle for what it was—recognition of her skill in getting people to talk freely to her.

"Okay," he said, "go ahead and try to talk to Brenda Simms. See if you can get her to remember whether she saw Sharon on the sixth. If she didn't, find out whether she knows anybody else who might have. It sounds like our Mrs Kolvek had some pretty dangerous habits. Maybe she got hold of the wrong man."

"Right. By the way, how'd the autopsy go?"

Randall groaned. "It sure was a good thing I didn't have any lunch. The only consolation is that Elizabeth Barron was right behind me in the run for the john. I've never seen a body in worse condition. She looked... Anyway, if you want to know whether we know more now than we did before the autopsy, the answer is not a hell of a lot. It probably happened five or six weeks ago, died from a massive blow to the head. We won't get the coroner's report for a couple weeks, par for the course. Our expert didn't want to commit himself either—not even to me, I wasn't asking for it in writing, for God's sake. He finally did say that the wound could have been accidental. It isn't outside the realm of possibility that it was self-inflicted, but that's pretty unlikely; she'd have had to be a contortionist.

"So anyway even though it's not a clean case for the D.A. it certainly isn't a pass. I think Elizabeth will try and convince the jurors that there's no reasonable doubt it was murder."

"So," Jenny said. "We're in high gear, right?"

"That's right."

She hung up and stood thinking for a moment. She would have to remember to cancel her dentist's appointment first thing in the morning. They'd probably charge her for it because it was such short notice, but disrupted schedules went with the territory.

AUTOPSY REPORT

OFFICE OF THE CORONER
County of San Marin

Name of Deceased:	SHARON SUSAN KOLVEK
Place of Death:	Found in forested area of San Marin County
Date of Death:	Found September 10, 1985
Place of Autopsy:	San Marin County Examining Room
Date of Autopsy:	September 17, 1985; 3:45 p.m.

EXTERNAL EXAMINATION

The remains are those of a Caucasian woman, and are in an advanced stage of decomposition and somewhat maggot-infested. Portions of the left side of the body reveal signs of animal teeth, but a determination as to what extent the condition of the body is due to animal feeding is impossible because of the degradation of body tissue by maggots and other insects. The frontal portion of the scalp is missing, revealing a calvarium showing a defect approximately six cm in diameter and one cm deep at its most concave point, with a thin-line fracture extending outward to the left parietal aspect at an oblique angle. The hair is mixed dark brown and gray. Small portions of foreign matter were removed from the hair and scalp in the area of the defect.

The chest cavity has been opened by resecting through the cartilaginous portions just to the left of the sternum. The abdomen is also open. Loops of bowel are identified. All extremities show extensive absence of skin with the absence of musculature on the more distal aspects.

INTERNAL EXAMINATION

Due to the extensive decomposition of the body it was infeasible to do separate respiratory, gastrointestinal, liver and biliary, pancreas, hematopoietic, and endocrine system examinations. The identifiable organs show extensive postmortem autolytic changes. No measurements or weights of lungs, kidneys, and liver were taken due to incomplete nature of these organs. The spleen is missing. There is no evidence of hemorrhage in any of the remaining organs. The larynx, together with its connective tissues, shows discoloration, the cause of which is undeterminable.

CARDIOVASCULAR SYSTEM

Multiple sections of the coronary arteries reveal no evidence of recent or old occlusion. The myocardium was not intact enough to allow for analysis. The same is true of the tricuspid and mitral valves, but pulmonic and aortic valves show no abnormality.

MUSCULOSKELETAL SYSTEM

The musculature which remains is consistent with that of an adult female.

The right tibia shows evidence of a previous fracture, at least ten years old. No other fractures are identified and the skeleton is consistent with that of an adult female.

CENTRAL NERVOUS SYSTEM

The portions of the scalp and facial tissue which remain are reflected. The maxilla is mobile. The zygomatic arches are intact. A defect of the frontal aspect has been previously noted, and in addition to the thin-line fracture noted the calvarium shows multiple small linear fractures in the area of the frontal defect. Removal of the roof of the calvarium exposes a small amount of softened and liquified brain tissue. Bone fragments from the area of defect are located within the cranial vault. The interior of the cranial vault is discolored.

CAUSE OF DEATH

Apparent cause of death is hemorrhage and pressure in cranial vault.

Cecelia Mayrick
CECILIA MAYRICK, M.D.
Pathologist for the Coroner

5

Randall noticed Roberts fidgeting restlessly in his chair at the defense table. He knew that his client only wanted to ask him what was going on, but he shook his head at him sharply, warning him silently to hold onto his questions until the sentencing hearing was over. Judge Aries was a holy terror on the bench, insisting on total silence in the courtroom, and Randall had no intention of jeopardizing in any way his client's slim chance to walk out a free man. The Nebraska prior had turned out to be unimportant: a juvenile shoplifting charge that shouldn't even have turned up on his permanent record. But Aries would still consider it.

The judge set down Randall's statement in mitigation and took his glasses off and put them on top of it. He rubbed his nose for a few moments and then looked directly at Roberts, who, as instructed, managed to meet his stare with a look of respect.

After a two-minute eternity the judge

looked down again at his papers and made his ruling.

"All right, gentlemen. Now I've listened to Mr. Cliffs here from the District Attorney's office tell me why I should put Mr Roberts in jail and throw away the key. And I've heard your arguments, Mr Randall, that your client should not do any time at all. And at this point I feel compelled to say that in my opinion, in my personal opinion, the world would certainly be a better place without Mr Roberts running around loose in it."

Roberts tensed up; Randall shot him a warning glance.

"However, my personal opinions are not what govern the rulings of this court; the law is what governs them. And in this instance I must reluctantly concede that Mr Randall is correct when he says that under Proposition Eight, the courts in this state are required to give tremendous weight to the question of restitution. And it is obvious that whatever chance the victims of this fraud have for restitution lie in Mr Roberts being able to make a success of the legitimate business he seems to be running as a sideline to his fraudulent enterprise."

Here the judge glared at Roberts, who could not force himself to meet his eyes. Randall sat stiffly at Roberts' side, almost afraid to breathe for fear of upsetting the delicate balance of his argument.

Judge Aries put on his glasses and

continued. "However, I'm not willing to let Mr Roberts think he's just going to walk away from this quarter-of-a-million dollar scheme. So I'm ordering that he serve one hundred and twenty days in the community work-furlough project. Mr Roberts will spend his nights in the work-furlough facility, and his days working to build his business, preparatory to making restitution of two hundred and fifty thousand dollars and paying a ten thousand dollar fine. At the end of the work furlough commitment, Mr Roberts will commence five hundred hours of volunteer community work during his free time. Maybe this schedule will keep him busy enough so that he can stay out of trouble.

"Mr Cliffs and Mr Randall, I will expect you back in court one week from today with a plan for restitution acceptable to the People and feasible for the defendant."

Randall and Cliffs murmured their acknowledgement and Judge Aries once again fixed his eyes on Roberts.

"As for you, Mr Roberts, I want you to know that I'll be monitoring this case very closely. If you fail to meet any of the requirements of this order which will be drawn up — even if your failure involves being one day late or one dollar short — I want you to know that I'll have you doing real time so fast you won't even have a chance to wipe off that grin I see forming on your face. Court is adjourned."

Randall stood up and nudged his client to do the same. He did not relax until the judge had left the courtroom. Before he could talk to Roberts, who was no longer smiling, Cliffs came up from the prosecutor's table to shake hands.

"I've got to admit that was a dynamite presentation, Jim. I thought for sure your client was looking at some hard time."

Randall grinned deprecatingly. "Well, now, Phil, I can't take all the credit. Most of it's got to go to the folks who wrote Proposition Eight: they left the barn door wide open. I just drove the buggy through."

"I'm not sure they'll want to take the credit for this one," Cliffs said dryly. "Anyway let me give you a call when I'm back in my office so we can set up a meeting to discuss this restitution thing."

"Sounds good." They shook hands again and Randall turned to Roberts as Cliffs walked away.

"You've got to go with the bailiff now to get processed, so we don't have any time to talk. I'll see you this afternoon."

While his client was being led out, he packed his briefcase, taking his time so that the spectators who had watched the proceedings would get tired of waiting for him and leave.

He felt good and whistled to himself as he swung down the courthouse corridor. If it wasn't so crowded he would have been swinging his briefcase as he walked. It seemed to him that everybody had won today. Roberts was by no means one of his favorite clients, but he seemed weak rather than malicious. And the fact remained that if the man had been locked up his family would have had to go on welfare, and the victims of his scheme would not have had any way to get their money back. Now the fine would help to reimburse the court system for the cost of the prosecution and the supervised probation. And restitution would most likely be made and Roberts would continue to support his family. The whole thing was a victory.

He felt ready to knock down mountains. Even the enervating heat didn't slow him down. He spotted a familiar brown pin-striped back in front of him, and quickened his step.

"Hey, Elizabeth."

She turned slightly, and he noticed her face harden for a moment when she saw him. But she recovered quickly and stopped to wait for him.

"Hi, Jim. You're looking pretty chipper in this weather."

"Oh, I'm a native. The heat doesn't get to me."

She smiled slightly. "Well, it gets to me. On days like this I wish I'd taken a job across the street."

The federal courthouse stood across the

street, in stark contrast to the county courthouse. It was new, it was clean, it was airy and it was air-conditioned. In the county building only seniority determined who got relief from the heat — in the form of first shot at the few elderly fans.

"I know what you mean," Randall said easily. Actually he was fond of the old building; his had been some of the footsteps that had worn down the tile over the years. He paused a moment, as though he were joining Elizabeth in contemplation of the cool federal hallways but he was timing their progress down the corridor. When he was ready, he said, "By the way, have you got a minute? I'd like to talk to you about the Kolvek investigation."

As he had expected her to, Elizabeth said quickly, "I'd like to, Jim, but this isn't really the right place. Why don't you call me so we can meet somewhere more privately? I'll be in and out most of the day, but keep trying..."

She broke off as Randall stopped walking. He smiled at her. "I see what you mean." He opened a door next to him. "But maybe if we could just take a minute now we could save ourselves a lot of time. Let's just pop into the attorney's lounge here for a minute."

He held the door open politely with one arm so that she could pass through.

She hesitated a moment, aware that she had been out-maneuvered. Then she gave a slight laugh, shook her head thoughtfully, and entered the lounge, which, as Randall had anticipated, was almost empty at this time of the day. Only one attorney was packing his briefcase, getting ready to leave. Randall nodded at him and walked over to the vending machine.

"Can I buy you a cup of coffee?" he asked Elizabeth.

She came over, silently produced her own quarter, gave the machine an expert kick in order to get what passed for cream, and then picked up her cup and walked, with Randall behind her, to a small table in the corner. He had manipulated her into this conversation, but it was apparent that she was not going to allow him to stampede her into telling him anything she wasn't ready for him to know.

Randall moved to the point.

"I've gotten copies of the autopsy and toxicology reports on Sharon Kolvek, but of course the coroner's isn't ready yet. Do you know when it will be? It's been two weeks now."

She sipped her coffee. Randall knew he was taking a risk forcing the issue this way, but he felt more comfortable talking to her face-to-face than on the telephone.

"I'm expecting it any day now," she said abruptly. "They expedited it for us. Anyway we both know what it will say. Cause of death was a heavy blow to the top of the head by a second party. Place of death unknown. Time of death between five and six weeks ago, closer to five."

"Hey," Randall said pleasantly, "what do you mean, a blow by a second party? My expert says the wound could have been accidental. Or self-inflicted."

She smiled genuinely at that. "Oh, come on, Jim. No, the coroner can't say it wasn't accidental or self-inflicted because he wasn't there when it happened. But there's a high degree of probability about what happened. You know as well as I do, that if it was self-inflicted, she'd have had to run her head full-tilt into a rock — and even if she would do that for any reason, which she wouldn't, the vertebrae trauma doesn't bear that out. Or else she turned herself upside down and dropped head-first onto a rock. Same objections.

"Of course, she could have just been walking along and a rock could have dropped on her head from out of the blue. You could try that on a jury if you want to."

She dropped the sarcastic tone and looked at him seriously.

"Now you know the problems. Where is the weapon? Where is the blood? Not in the trench where she was found. Somebody moved her after she died, Jim. And we have to proceed on the assumption that the person who moved her is the same person who killed her. Right now that's an assumption, but I think pretty soon we'll be able to prove it."

She sat back and picked up her coffee cup again. She didn't seem anxious any longer to get away. She had given him some information. Now she was waiting for the *quid pro quo.*

"Okay, I think I understand your premise. I have just two problems with it. First, why do you keep talking about a rock?"

Barron gestured impatiently. "When you get the coroner's report you'll see why. Fragments of a rock of a soft, porous nature were found in the wound. 'Soft' is a relative term, of course. It was hard enough to split her skull open."

Randall nodded slowly. "You also said 'you'—meaning me—could pitch it to the jury. I represent Joseph Kolvek in this case, and I won't be representing anyone else. So it sounds to me like you've already decided he's guilty. Can I assume you haven't got an open mind while this investigation is pending?"

She flushed, and said stiffly, "You're right. This case is still in an investigative stage and my phrasing was improper. I apologize."

Randall shook his head sharply. "I don't care about that, Elizabeth. This isn't on the public record. I just want to know why you're so sure. And thanks for the apology, but you are sure. You've already made up your mind. And I want to know why."

Stubbornly she repeated, "This case is still in an investigative stage. When we have any proof of guilt, we'll file a complaint and if you are the attorney of record for the accused, you'll be entitled to know what we have."

Randall decided to try and startle something out of her. "But you are looking very closely at my client, more than is justified by the fact that he's the husband of the deceased. Why? Do you have anything more concrete to go on than Elaine Morris's whisperings behind the scene?"

Her eyes narrowed. "What do you mean by that comment? I've never said anything like that, and I'm sure Bud hasn't either. Who'd you get that from?"

He had certainly gotten a reaction, but he didn't know yet what he could do with it. Barron was rattled because there seemed to be a leak in the office. He didn't want her fastening onto the details of the leak and trying to get a name out of him. Even if he were disposed to give it to her, which he was emphatically not, he couldn't. He didn't know who had told Jenny, and he had been very careful not to ask.

He tried to prod her back onto the track. "It wasn't too hard to find out what set the D.A.'s office onto the trail so quickly. But you wouldn't be pushing this so hard if you didn't have something more. If you're chasing a red herring, I'd like a chance to respond on behalf of my client, that's all. It could save us all a lot of time and money."

She shook her head. He knew he wasn't

going to get any more out of her. He was disappointed, but he couldn't help admiring her quick recovery from what had obviously been an unpleasant surprise for her.

She stood up and picked up her briefcase. "Well," she said, "it's been interesting. If things do progress to the stage where we're ready to get an arrest warrant for your client, I'll be sure to let you know."

Randall thanked her, although they both knew her offer was simply standard professional courtesy. She walked away and then stopped, just before the door.

"I don't think it will hurt you to tell you one thing we've uncovered. We've got a witness who saw a man carrying a large bundle, about the size and shape of a body, out of the Kolvek house late on the night of August sixth or early on the morning of August seventh. It was dark and the witness couldn't see all that clearly, but as far as I'm concerned that's enough for us to be giving some nitpicking scrutiny to your client."

Randall leapt to his feet. "What witness?" But the door was already swinging shut behind Elizabeth Barron. He couldn't very well run down the halls yelling after her.

And he didn't think she would tell him any more even then. She had told him just what she wanted him to know and nothing more. In fact, he began to wonder who had manipulated whom in this interview.

Sally was just hanging up the phone as he walked in the door. "So," she said, "how did it go?"

He waved his hand in the air. "Little bit good, little bit bad."

She followed him into his office.

"Are you going to tell me what that means?"

He snapped open his briefcase latches. "I ran into Elizabeth Barron in the courthouse. First, have you heard from Jenny yet today? Has she been able to contact that Simms woman?"

"No, but she did call this morning to say Simms has been out of town. She's due back at the end of the week."

"And the neighborhood canvas?"

"Still nothing. By the way, while we're on the Kolvek case, those charge slips came in from Mastercard and Visa. We haven't got the others yet."

He raised his eyebrows. "In just ten working days? That must be some kind of a record."

"We asked them to expedite and I guess they actually did. What do you want me to do with them?"

"I'm going to dictate a letter and we're going to send them over to Shallot, along with a specimen of Kolvek's handwriting."

"Oho," Sally said. "Light dawns."

Shallot was a handwriting expert and now Sally knew why Randall had not sent the information about the charge slips right over to the D.A.'s office. He wanted to be sure first that Kolvek had not forged his wife's name. That alone would have indicated his guilt. And a large part of Randall's job was protecting his clients from their own stupidity. He had to check everything his clients had told him before he could present it in evidence.

"So then if Shallot says it's not Kolvek's writing, we'll give them to the D.A.?"

Randall sank slowly into his chair. "Well, that's something I'm going to have to think about. I've got the feeling Elizabeth Barron is going to file on Kolvek no matter what I come up with — unless maybe it's a signed confession from somebody else. So it might not do any good to present it now. I may just hang onto it . . . if we get to a preliminary hearing it might shake the probable cause standard enough for us to get a dismissal."

He rocked back thoughtfully in his chair for a minute. Then he sat up. "I'll decide about that later," he said briskly. "What I need right now is a way to break up this logjam we've run into on the flow of information. So what I think we need is a meeting with the Kolvek family. Why don't you get Kolvek on the line for me? And get Jenny too. I'd like her to be there as a witness. Tell her I'll try to get it set up for tonight or tomorrow night at Kolvek's house."

"Right," Sally said. "Oh and by the way, what happened to Roberts?"

Randall looked blank for a moment and then he laughed. "God, I forgot all about him. We got him a ten thousand dollar fine, full restitution, community work and some work furlough time."

"But that's fantastic!"

Randall said ruefully, "Aries didn't think so. You should have seen his face while he made the ruling. He looked like he was sucking a lemon." He grinned. "It's a real pleasure to know that I have good news to give Mrs Roberts. Too bad I didn't get to enjoy it a while longer before Elizabeth brought me down."

They both knew there was never enough time to savor the victories before the next brushfire broke out.

CORONER'S REPORT

OFFICE OF THE CORONER
County of San Marin

File Number:	07124E49
Name of Deceased:	Sharon Susan Kolvek
Residence:	13127 Reyna Way
Place of Death:	Body found in forested area 10 miles NNW of county line
Date of Death:	Body found September 10, 1985
Informant:	San Marin County Sheriff's Department
Deputy Coroner:	H. L. Monteer
Person Notified:	Joseph Kolvek
Relationship:	Husband

INVESTIGATIVE SUMMARY:

The undersigned viewed the decedent supine on a gurney in the Coroner's facility. The remains were in an advanced stage of decomposition and were partially skeletonized. An extensive fracture was noted in the frontal region of the skull. The remains were those of an adult female. Identification was established through dental records.

Investigation by the undersigned revealed that the decedent's daughter, Elaine Morris, had on August 12, 1985 filed a missing persons report with the San Marin County Sheriff's Department in which she indicated the decedent had been missing since August 7.

Officer G. F. Roya (I.D. Number 1823F) of the San Marin County Sheriff's Department related the decedent's remains had been found at approximately 2:35 p.m. on September 10 in a heavily wooded area in the eastern portion of the county, approximately ten miles north-northwest of the easternmost county line. Tentative identification had been made by decedent's husband, Joseph Kolvek.

For further information regarding this case, please refer to the District Attorney's Investigative Unit, report number 93-1A29.

An autopsy and laboratory studies revealed that the exact cause of death was undeterminable, but that the high probability was death had been caused by a single blow to the frontal bone of the skull. Particles of foreign matter recovered from the area of the fracture have been revealed under preliminary analysis to be debris of a soft, porous rock of sedimentary origins.

Due to the position of the fracture and other external factors, it is the position of the coroner's office that the probability factors are high that this blow was neither self-inflicted nor the result of an accidental fall.

H. L. Monteer

H. L. MONTEER, Deputy Coroner

6

The Kolvek house looked, if possible, even better than it had the first time Randall had seen it. "My gosh," Jenny said, suitably impressed.

Shards of sunlight danced off the delicately etched window panes across the front of the house, and the whole building glowed in the setting sun. Kolvek had said that this house was part of a development and the entire neighborhood had been nothing but scrubweed as recently as seven years ago. But anything less like a tract house would be hard to imagine.

The small parking area to the side of the garage was already filled. Randall parked in the gravel driveway. He made a mental bet with himself that the battered Volkswagen bug belonged to Thomas Kolvek and that the immaculate Mercedes was Elaine Morris's. By default the Cherokee Renegade must be Susan Jordan's. Joseph Kolvek's car was undoubtedly in the garage; it must be some kind of functional heavy American car.

"So," he said to Jenny, continuing the conversation they had had on the drive over, "you haven't any idea about the D.A.'s mystery witness."

"No. I've hit almost every house in the neighborhood. I've even walked around here late at night on the chance it could have been someone walking his dog. Maybe the D.A. is just bluffing, have you thought of that?"

Randall's fingers drummed absently on the steering wheel. "I don't know," he said. "I don't think it's Elizabeth's style to bluff on something so basic as this. But you're right, I can't understand why the witness hasn't come to light for us. I mean, you said everybody's pretty cooperative here."

He knew from experience that people in "old money" sections of town, and, conversely, people in the poorest sections, tended to keep their mouths and eyes wilfully closed unless a badge forced them open. But Jenny had found the people here to be helpful; they seemed interested rather than repelled, possibly because the crime, if any, had taken place a while ago.

Something moved in the house; Randall looked over and saw Kolvek opening the front door. "Here we go," he said to Jenny and they slid out of the car.

Kolvek nodded at them and stood aside without speaking while they went through the door, after a brief moment of confusion while Jenny hung back to let her boss go through, and Randall tried to let the lady precede him. Kolvek, never the soul of patience, let the door go and walked ahead of them down the hallway. Randall followed him and Jenny took up the rear.

Four pairs of eyes, two of them actively hostile, gazed at them from a living room which had undergone a pleasant change. The rigid furniture groupings had been broken up into more relaxed seating arrangements, and the angles of the sofas and chairs were softened by some attractive throw pillows. The heavy draperies had been taken off the windows; only sheer curtains remained, brightening the room with filtered sunlight.

Unfortunately the pleasant atmosphere was not reflected in the faces which now confronted Randall. "This is my oldest daughter, Elaine Morris," Kolvek said. Randall took the limp hand rather reluctantly offered by a smartly dressed thirtyish woman with a rigid hairdo and just a dab of lipstick. Her eyes narrowed when Kolvek called her "oldest"; otherwise her face was carefully blank.

"My son-in-law, Raymond Morris." A rather short and very bald man standing at the far side of the room next to a drinks trolley saluted Randall with his glass.

"My other daughter, Susan Jordan." A dark-haired woman, rather harried-looking, in black slacks and a blue knit top, was the first person in the room to smile at him. Her handclasp was firm.

"I appreciate your coming here tonight," Randall said to her gratefully. "I understand that your schedule is pretty crowded."

Her smile widened. "That's one way to put it, yes. Three kids, assorted dogs, cats and gerbils and my husband's trying to get his business going—he's an accountant. I'm trying to help him and all that doesn't give me a lot of leisure time."

"Well, if Don had stayed with Central Services he'd be a vice president by now, then you'd be able to afford a babysitter so he could be here with you tonight," Elaine Morris said.

Susan Jordan's gaze wandered over to Raymond Morris. "Oh, I don't know," she said. "Sometimes husbandly support isn't all it's cracked up to be."

Elaine turned red. Before she could answer, Kolvek said calmly, "And you've met Thomas," nodding toward his son, who sat on the sofa in a corner of the room, away from the others. After a pause Kolvek added, "I'd apologize for his manners, but I've given up doing that."

Flushing painfully, Thomas Kolvek rose, nodded stiffly at Randall and then resumed his seat. He was a good-looking young man in a passive way, despite his bad complexion and pathetic attempt at a moustache. He seemed unfortunately to have chosen a sullen attitude as his weapon against his older sister's aggressive personality and his father's cool confidence.

Randall sat down; Jenny had taken a seat in an unobtrusive corner from which she could watch the scene.

"Now," Elaine Morris said, "why don't we get right to the point? I think we've all talked to the prosecutor's office already and I don't see what purpose is going to be served by this meeting."

"Well," Randall replied mildly, "I'm just trying to get your different views on what might have happened to your mother. I know you've already discussed this with the D.A.'s office, but they aren't taking me into their confidence about what you've told them. I think we have to start out with the premise that I don't know anything."

He sensed that Elaine Morris was relieved that he knew nothing about what she had said to the D.A.'s office. She was undoubtedly not anxious for her father to know the extent to which she had involved herself in the case. She was therefore slightly off balance. He wanted to keep her there, so he intended to ignore her and question the other members of the family.

Kolvek stood in his usual position at the side of the fireplace, staring into the empty grate. He was detaching himself from the conversation, as Randall had advised him to do over the phone. There might be some interesting revelations as the meeting heated up, but Randall did not want those revelations coming from his client.

"Now," Randall said briskly, "let me summarize what I know about the last time you were all together with your mother. It was at a family dinner in the early part of August. There was an argument during dinner, and shortly after dinner Mrs Jordan and her family left, followed by the Morris family. Thomas Kolvek stayed a while, and then he left too."

He paused, looking around the room. It seemed to him that Susan Jordan's emotional investment in the discussion was relatively slight, so he decided to start his questioning with her.

"Mrs Jordan, is that how you remember it?"

"I suppose so. It didn't stick in my mind."

He looked at her with some surprise. "It didn't stick in your mind even though it was the last time you saw your mother?"

She looked around a little nervously. "Well, listen, at the time I couldn't know it was going to be the last time, could I?"

"But to the best of your recollection now, that dinner in early August was the last time you saw your mother?"

"I don't remember the date, but if you say it was early August I suppose that's when it was."

"August sixth," Elaine Morris said.

"Okay," Susan said. "If Elaine says it was August sixth, it probably was. I can't remember after all this time. I don't keep a social calendar."

Obviously that was a telling blow at Elaine. Susan went blandly on. "I don't remember anything special about that evening, if that's what you want to know. We don't have a lot of family get-togethers, and in fact we haven't had one since that night. But when we did get together it was usually for dinner and it was usually here. I don't know what we ate that night, or even what we talked about.

"I do remember vaguely that Elaine called me a couple of days later and asked me if I had talked to Ma. She said she hadn't been able to get hold of her. I didn't pay any particular attention because I figured my mother was just trying to avoid Elaine."

She paused and then went impassively on, a true Kolvek after all.

"Well, I did start to get a little concerned when I hadn't heard from my mother for over a week. We're not a close family, but Ma did check every once in a while to see how we were doing. So I called Dad and he told me he hadn't heard from her since the night of the dinner. He just assumed she'd taken off again."

Randall caught her up. "Again? You

mean she had gone off before without letting anybody know?"

She hesitated. "Well, yes, but those times she'd give one of us a call and say she couldn't stand it for another moment and she was going to get away for a while." She glanced at her father who stood inscrutable as usual.

"Do you know where she usually went on those occasions?"

"Usually back East to visit relatives. Once or twice she called Thomas and asked him to drive her up to the cabin. She didn't like driving on those winding roads."

"But to the best of your knowledge this time none of the family had heard from her, is that correct?"

"That's right. I called Thomas and he said he hadn't heard anything, and then I called Elaine. That's when she told me she was going to file a missing persons report. Then the sheriff's department called me — I guess they were following up on Elaine's call to them. Then ... Dad called me and told me they'd found a body near the cabin."

She fell silent. Randall was aware that Elaine Morris, sitting next to him, was expecting his questions. So he turned his attention next to Thomas.

"You stayed in the house for a little while after your sisters left on the sixth?"

"Yes." The young man seemed inclined

to leave it at that. Randall had no intention of having to ask the right questions to draw out monosyllabic answers from Thomas. Accordingly he waited, gazing steadily at Kolvek's son. Thomas began to fidget and then he started talking.

"I told you, I didn't stay long. There wasn't any reason to; neither one of them was in any mood to listen to what I had to say. So I left about fifteen minutes after Susan and Elaine. I told you all this before."

"Oh, you met before?" Elaine said.

Randall continued to ignore her.

"What did you want to say to your parents?" he asked Thomas.

He shook his head. "Nothing that could be of any relevance here," he said, and shut his mouth tightly. Muscles played in his jaw.

Randall prodded him. "Why don't you let me be the judge of that? You never know what might turn out to be important."

Thomas shook his head again. "It was strictly personal. I don't want to get into it, and I don't intend to."

Randall hesitated. Suddenly Elaine laughed loudly.

"Oh, Lord," she said, "don't tell me you were going to start in about owning your own restaurant again! Even if you could get him — " she indicated her father with a jerk of her head " — to give you the money for it, you know damn well you couldn't make a go of it."

Randall was becoming disgusted with the way members of this family cut at each other, but he said nothing and instead watched Thomas, who flushed dark red and jumped to his feet.

"What do you know about anything?" he shouted at Elaine. "Just because your own so-perfect life has turned out to be not so great, you get all your kicks out of knocking people who are still trying to make it!"

He looked furiously at Raymond Morris, who was swishing ice cubes in his drink, apparently oblivious to the tempest swirling around him.

Elaine rallied quickly after a startled pause. "I don't know what you're getting so nasty about. I'm just telling you for your own good that in my opinion you aren't cut out to be an entrepreneur. Mother knew it too; that's why she never backed you up when you asked for money. I think you know as well as the rest of us that you're damned lucky to have a father who can give you a job."

For a moment Randall was concerned that Thomas might actually choke on his rage. The meeting was getting out of hand. The lawyer was relieved when Susan Jordan threw some cold water on the fire.

"I don't think any of us can know whether Thomas could or could not run a business. Right now he doesn't have any capital and it's obvious that Dad isn't about to give him any. So all this stuff is really beside the point."

Thomas's face began to regain its normal pallor. He shot a glance at his father, who still stood looking into the grate, and muttered, "I know I could make it, if I just got a break. It's not like I'm asking for a gift; I'm just asking for a loan."

"It doesn't matter what you call it," Susan Jordan said firmly. "You know the rules. Dad didn't give any money to Don and me and he's not going to make an exception in your case. I don't know why you keep fighting the same old battle over and over again."

Enraged afresh, Thomas burst out again. "That's so damn unfair! Why should we have to wait until he's dead to—" As his brain suddenly seemed to hear what his tongue was saying, he shut up and sank back again onto his sofa. The room became completely silent. Kolvek turned slowly away from the fireplace to look at his son.

After a minute he said calmly, "When you've worked for thirty years to build something, then maybe I'll consider giving you a loan. Otherwise you'll all have to wait until I die so I can leave it to you in my will. *If* I leave it to you in my will."

"And who else are you going to leave it to?" Elaine Morris asked sharply. "We're all the family you've got. Who do you want to leave it to, a home for stray cats?"

Kolvek nodded calmly. "Its true. Right now you're all the family I've got."

"That's right!" she said. "So don't try to tell us—" she stopped, her eyes narrowed. "What do you mean, 'right now'?"

Kolvek did not reply.

"We're getting off the point," Susan Jordan said irritably. "None of this has anything to do with what happened to Ma."

"Will you stop calling Mother that?" Elaine Morris snapped at her. "It sounds so vulgar!"

Susan Jordan looked at her coldly. "You know, Elaine, you've got a real problem. You can't change Ma by calling her 'Mother'. She came from the wrong side of the tracks and she never pretended to be anything she wasn't. She thought your affectations were just a big hoot."

She stood up and spoke to Randall. "I'm sorry to break this up, if you had more questions, but I've got to get home. Don isn't too good at making the kids stay in bed once he finally gets them there." She looked at her brother. "Thomas, I saw your VW out there, but if it's not running right, I'll be glad to give you a lift home."

"No," he said. "It's running fine. But it's time I was going too."

Susan nodded and gathered up her purse and keys. She called good-night to her father. Even this preferred daughter did not make any move to touch her father physically.

Elaine rose too. "Come on," she said to her husband, who was staring into space. She went over and took the half-empty glass from his hand. "It's time to go." She glanced coldly at Randall. "So long," she said.

Randall heard the two sisters speaking civilly to each other as they left the house. It was amazing that they could decompress so quickly from their emotional confrontation. This came from long practice, no doubt. Thomas Kolvek glanced at Randall and followed his sisters out without speaking.

The room was suddenly quiet. Randall dropped into a chair, feeling slightly shell-shocked. Jenny's face was impassive and so, as usual, was Kolvek's.

"Would you mind taking a little stroll outside, Jenny? I'd like to talk to Mr Kolvek for a minute."

Randall braced himself to try and pry out some answers to the questions which the family meeting had raised.

LAST WILL AND TESTAMENT

I, Mikael Kolvek, being of sound mind and body, do hereby make my last will and testament as follows:

I give everything I have to my son, Joseph William Kolvek, with the understanding that if I die before my wife Joseph is to take care of his mother just as I would have had I been alive.

Dated: January 24, 1949

Mikael Kolvek

WITNESSED.

Sandra Janis
James Mikelek

7

Kolvek walked over to the trolley. "Can I get you anything to drink?"

"Yes, please. Bourbon and water," Randall said.

Kolvek deftly put the drink together for Randall and uncapped a bottle of beer for himself.

Randall located his notes from the talk with Elizabeth Barron. He took a sip of his drink and put it down on the coffee table in front of him. "Okay," he said. "You remember I told you on the phone that I've talked to Elizabeth Barron from the D.A.'s office. I'm afraid she gave me bad news. There isn't any doubt that they're planning to file charges against you. I don't think they're going through the grand jury, presumably because they know I'll just demand a preliminary hearing anyway."

He paused. Kolvek was back standing at the fireplace with his beer. He took a long, calm drink.

"So far as I can tell, they're not considering any other suspects," Randall said. "That's what we have to fight. You're the obvious suspect, because the husband always is the obvious suspect. Unless we can come up right away with some solid evidence either that your wife wasn't actually murdered or that someone else did it, you can bet that they'll file against you in the next couple of days."

He paused again. "Wouldn't you like to sit down?" he asked.

"I'm fine," Kolvek said.

"Well, let's take it worst case," Randall said. "Let's assume you get charged and go on trial for murder. Now the D.A. is taking the position that the coroner's report indicates death from a blow on the head which was neither accidental nor self-inflicted. We've got some room to manoeuvre there, because the coroner hasn't made the statement with one hundred percent certainty. We've got our own expert and we can hammer at the fact that due to the nature of the fracture and the decomposed condition of the body, there is room for some doubt. That's a point in our favor. Of course, against that you have to bear in mind that sometimes juries are turned off by medical experts, and also they tend to give the coroner's office more weight than they give an independent consultant like our forensic pathologist.

"So if it gets to the point where we have

to convince a jury, we'll have to come up with a realistic scenario to pitch to them; we have to find some way Sharon Kolvek could have died besides the theory that the D.A.'s office is going to advance."

Randall suddenly remembered that he was talking about Joseph Kolvek's wife; he stopped, appalled at his callousness. But Kolvek demonstrated no emotion; they might just as well have been discussing whether to build a redwood or a cedar fence. Randall sighed softly, took another sip of his drink, and went on.

"I picked up a copy of the coroner's report before I came here tonight, and as I say, there's some room to manoeuvre. Everybody thinks it's murder because it's obvious that the body was moved after the blow. Now with some head wounds it's not impossible that the victim can walk around afterwards; conceivably even drive a car. But from what Dr Emery — that's our forensic expert — from what he tells me, in this case that would be really reaching.

"The coroner's office has said that the blow was struck with a soft, porous rock. I don't think the D.A.'s office expects to find the weapon and I haven't heard that they're making any effort in that direction. At the moment we're still maintaining the polite fiction that I just represent you as the husband of the deceased and the coroner's office has been very cooperative; they let me have samples of all the cuttings and scrapings for our own analysis. If you were just an ordinary suspect, I couldn't have done that without a court order, which the D.A.'s office would probably have tried to stop. So that's one thing that's worked to our advantage."

He paused again, took a drink and said hopefully, "Please don't hesitate to stop me if you have any questions or comments, or if there's something that you don't understand. I'm telling you all this so that you'll know exactly where you stand right now, and what you probably have to look forward to in the next couple of weeks. There's no point in all this if it isn't perfectly clear to you, or if there's something I've overlooked."

Kolvek nodded.

Randall resigned himself to continuing his monologue. He was getting sick of the sound of his own voice. "Getting back to the blow. Briefly, it was apparently a heavy, kind of smooth rock. I assume it broke the skin — it's not possible any longer to tell. But it wasn't jagged enough to put a hole in the skull. It created a hair-line fracture at the point of impact... I don't mean to be offensive, or upset you, but you'll hear all this anyway if we go to court, and I want you to know exactly what's going on. Now the skull was depressed at the fracture point, creating pressure which caused heavy bleeding in the braincase. This was the presumed cause of death. In legal terms the bleeding was the immediate cause, but the skull depression was the proximate cause and so whatever caused the depression was also the proximate cause. The D.A. is going to allege that a blow struck by you, deliberately and with premeditation, was the proximate cause of death. And that's first degree murder.

"Now, since the fracture is centralized in the frontal area of the skull, at the hairline, the blow had to have been struck from the front, at a downward angle. It really is very hard to see how she could have done that herself, unless she ran forward, right into the rock. But the condition of the neck vertebrae, which were relatively intact, was not consistent with a forward motion brought to an abrupt halt. It was more consistent with her standing up at the time of impact."

Kolvek spoke for the first time. "How can they know something like that?"

Pleased that Kolvek was listening and responding, Randall leaned forward intently. "That's relatively simple. If she were running leaning forward, and she slammed into a solid obstruction, the force of the impact would result in a compression of the cartilege between the vertebrae all down her back. On the other hand, if she received a blow from in front and slightly above her, her head would snap back and there would be an entirely different trauma pattern along the vertebrae. Now that's just a layman's explanation; it would sound entirely different if the D.A. put a doctor on the stand to explain it to the jury. But that's the gist of it. Does that answer your question?"

Kolvek nodded slowly. He seemed to be turning it over in his mind. Randall had the impression that something was wrong. Suddenly he remembered that Kolvek had had only a seventh-grade education. The man was so confident and self-possessed that it was easy to forget that. Randall kept his eyes on his notes and said, choosing his words carefully, "Now as we know, the vertebrae are the building blocks of the spine. You can feel them, those bumps down the center of your back. Now you can understand that they will react to the way the blow was struck."

He looked up and saw that Kolvek's face had cleared. He breathed a silent sigh of relief that they had made it over that hurdle. It occurred to him for the first time that Kolvek's stolidity and impassivity in the face of grim and devastating news might reflect not inhuman detachment, but rather a fear of showing his ignorance. He decided not to go into any more anatomical detail for the moment.

"So anyway I'm saying basically that if we're going to go with the defense that it was an accident, we need to come up with something very simple. We could say that she was walking forward and she accidentally walked into an overhanging rock, but that wouldn't explain the force of the impact, or even why she would do such a thing. Why wouldn't she see the rock? Or—" he smiled wryly "—the rock could have fallen on her, but where would it come from? Juries aren't going to strain themselves trying to accept peculiar explanations; almost always they go with the obvious. So that's where we stand right now. Okay?"

Kolvek thought for a while and then nodded. "I think I understand. From what you say, I'm going on trial real soon. Is that right?"

"No, no." Randall shook his head vehemently. "Not at all. I should have explained to begin with that we're discussing the status of the evidence as it exists right now, and how that evidence will appear to a jury if the thing gets that far. I don't mean to say that it definitely will get that far or that if it does, the trial is right around the corner. You haven't even been charged yet. *If* you are, *when* you are, we still have to go through the arraignment in the Municipal Court, we have to go through initial motions, a preliminary hearing, a second arraignment in the Superior Court if you're bound over, pretrial motions, a readiness conference—and then trial only after all that."

Kolvek nodded, silent again.

"Now I've talked to Elizabeth Barron—from the D.A.'s office—and she has agreed to let me know when she gets an arrest warrant for you, which means that the sheriff's people will not come out here to your house and pick you up and take you to the county jail. We'll make arrangements to surrender you in court on the day of the arraignment. At that time bail will be fixed and with luck you'll be booked in the morning and be out in the afternoon. Still with me?"

Kolvek nodded again, but Randall noticed that he was gripping the mantelpiece so hard that the muscles of his upper arm bulged against his shirt sleeve. Most people were intimidated by the machinery of the law, and probably this was magnified in Kolvek's case. It was all totally unfamiliar to him, and, in addition, words were not his forte and Randall had thrown a lot of them at him this evening. It was hard to tell how much had actually been absorbed.

Randall got up to freshen his drink, and give Kolvek time to collect himself. He ran over in his mind what he had said, trying to remember if he had used any incomprehensible terms. It was difficult to put things simply and yet avoid sounding condescending to this client who had proven, many times in his career, just how shrewd he was.

Back in his seat, Randall asked, "Do you understand now what's going to be happening in the next couple of weeks? We can discuss the details of things as they happen, but is it clear what's on the burner now?"

"I think so. The prosecutor's going to file charges, she'll let you know and we're going into court for a hearing where the judge will set bail."

"Well yes, that's the general idea. But the purpose of the hearing is not just to set the bail. It's called an arraignment. They'll read the charges against you, they'll tell you your constitutional rights and you'll plead not guilty. Okay?"

"Yes," Kolvek said. "There is one thing I'd like to ask you about, though. Why is everybody so anxious to think I might have killed Sharon? Is it because we had a few fights?"

Randall shuffled through his papers for a moment, giving himself time to frame his answer.

"You have to understand that motive doesn't have to be proved," he said finally. "But juries like it and I assume in this case the prosecutor will be saying that you didn't want to share your assets with her, which you would have to do if there was a divorce. Or of course they could say that you lost your temper and acted in the heat of anger, but that would make it second degree, so they're probably not going to go for that right now."

Kolvek sat slowly down in an armchair. "I don't know about the heat of anger, although I will say that if I hadn't done it before this, I don't know why they'd think I'd do it now. But as far as not wanting to share community property, that's no reason. It don't amount to that much."

Kolvek's grammar had slipped; possibly a sign of agitation. But Randall found his statement astonishing. "But Mr Kolvek," he said, "this house alone must be worth a quarter of a million. Naturally, I don't know what loans are outstanding against it. And then there's Kolvek Construction."

Kolvek shook his head. "Uh uh. Almost all of this is mine."

Randall frowned. "Are you sure about that? Of course you know that California is a community property state." He began to consider how to explain community property to a man who had undoubtedly been brought up to believe that a man's property was his alone, and that a woman's property was also his.

But it was not necessary. Kolvek said, "Yes, I know that. But most of this I inherited from my father. You can talk to Eden about that. He set it all up for me."

Randall gazed at him thoughtfully. "I'd like to get this point clear as soon as I can. Do you happen to have Eden's home number?"

Kolvek nodded and went to get his address book. He read off the number to Randall. The phone rang a few times and then it was picked up and a hearty voice said, "Hotel Tequila Sunrise." Randall could hear music and laughter in the background.

"Hi Bill," he said. "Is that you?" He grinned and leaned back in his chair. "It's Jim Randall, Bill. You think you could tear yourself away from the party long enough to give me some information on the Kolvek estate?"

"Oh Jesus, hold on," Eden said. There was a complicated set of clickings as he moved to another phone and when he finally settled down the party noises had been shut off. "Don't you know it's the cocktail hour, Jim? Okay, never mind, I don't know why criminal lawyers are always in such a hurry. Okay, what can I tell you?"

"Well, I'm sitting here in the Kolvek house and Mr Kolvek has just told me that most of his assets are his separate property. You want to clarify that for me?" He added quickly, "Briefly. I don't need a lot of detail right now."

Eden sounded exasperated. "Listen, it took me, two associates, four paralegals and a bunch of law clerks almost six months to put it all together, and you want me to tell you all about it right now?"

"Actually, no," Randall said smoothly, "I don't want you to tell me all about it. All I want is a quick summary of the end result."

"You like to live dangerously, don't you?" Eden said. "Okay, then, listen carefully and don't interrupt, because I don't want to have to repeat anything. A few years ago Kolvek's father died, and left him the family farm in Michigan." He added parenthetically, "God, Jim, you should have seen that will. Fortunately there weren't any other relatives besides the mother. Otherwise I don't think we could have gotten it through probate in Michigan. Anyway, Kolvek asked me at the time what his status was and I told him that generally any inheritance is the separate property of the heir, particularly if it can be demonstrated that there was never any intention that the spouse share in the benefits. Of course any community money that is put into the inheritance starts a community property interest.

"It was a hundred acres of farm land; it wasn't worth much on the market from what I heard. But Kolvek wanted it kept separate. So we got some affadavits from people that Sharon Kolvek and Kolvek's father had hated each other, never got along. So then I arranged to sell a small part of it to Calhoun County for an easement, and we paid back taxes and probate fees out of that money. About eighteen months later, I think it was, Kolvek sold the land to some developers for a *very* good price. So we orchestrated the dissolution of the existing construction company—we put a fair price on the fixtures and good will and everything and we also valued everything else the Kolveks owned jointly, and called that community property. Mrs Kolvek got half the value of the community property in cash and she signed an agreement that everything else belonged separately to Joseph Kolvek. We put everything in his name, and re-formed Kolvek Construction, and that's the whole thing in a nutshell.

"Of course, now it's been five years, and some community property interest has built up again, but it's minimal, compared to the overall value. I consider it a completely legal, valid document. Of course you can sue anybody for anything—and who knows which way a judge is going to jump these days? Now I certainly hope that answers your questions because I'm the host here and I'm going back to my party."

He hung up, not bothering to say goodbye. Randall put down the receiver, and looked thoughtfully at Kolvek.

"Well," he said, "that would certainly seem to pull the rug out from under that motive. Unless of course they try to make a case out that because of your—uh—somewhat—traditional values, you couldn't accept the idea of a divorce... It doesn't sound too reasonable to claim that you'd rather murder your wife than divorce her. Of course people don't always act rationally. If they did, I'd be out of a job."

He expected no answer from Kolvek, and he didn't get one. He checked his preview sheet made out for this conference. He had hit all the necessary points but one. "Just one more thing. If you had to speculate about what happened to your wife, what would you say?" He held up his hand. "Now think. I really must have an answer to that question. Assuming it wasn't an accident, how do you think she might have ended up in that ditch?"

Kolvek picked up his empty beer bottle and rolled it between his palms. Several minutes elapsed before he answered.

"If I had to guess — and I don't like to — I'd say she played around with one man too many and he turned on her."

Randall knew how hard it must be for a man like Kolvek to admit to anyone what his wife had been, but he kept any hint of sympathy out of his voice. "Yes, we've had a few indications that that might have been it. I just wanted to make sure you couldn't give me another trail to follow."

He packed up his briefcase, and got briskly to his feet. "Well, I think I'd better go look for poor Jenny. She's been waiting all this time."

Kolvek nodded toward the French windows. "We can go out that way. I saw her walk past about five minutes ago."

There was a small stone patio outside the window; Randall stopped for a moment to enjoy the late summer sunset. Standing there, it was hard to believe that people lived anywhere within a mile of this place, it was so quiet and peaceful, hemmed in with tall trees. There was no swimming pool, but in a setting of warm stone pavement and flowering plants was an unexpected little waterfall which appeared to flow naturally into a crystal clear pool.

"This is really charming," Randall said.

"Well, that was the idea," Kolvek said. He gave a rare smile. "I've always liked the sound of running water."

"So you planned it? It didn't come with the house?"

"I built it," Kolvek said. "No, it didn't come with the house. I told you. This and the fireplace. I built them myself."

No doubt about it. Kolvek was a clever, sensitive craftsman, even though his taste in interior decoration was a little unpredictable.

"Well, you did a great job," Randall said. "I hope Jenny saw this. I guess she must have gone back to the car."

They began to walk toward the driveway. Without looking at him, Kolvek said in a quiet voice, "You've never asked me whether I did it."

Randall shook his head. "I know I haven't, and I won't. This might sound strange to you, but it really isn't any of my business. My job is to make sure that your rights are protected. I won't lie for you, I won't help you lie in court, I won't breach professional ethics or break laws. But what I will do is force the prosecution to prove their allegations every step of the way, so that you have the benefit of every legal right. I believe in that, preserving people's rights."

"You don't really care, do you?" Kolvek

sounded uncomprehending and a little bitter.

Randall stopped walking and turned to face him. "That depends on whether you're talking personally or professionally. Personally, of course it matters to me. But professionally it's not my job to find out. I'm not setting myself up as a judge or jury. They have their jobs, I have mine. I'm just one link in a chain, Mr Kolvek."

They walked on again in silence. Jenny was indeed sitting in the car. Randall held his hand out to Kolvek.

"Thanks for the drinks," he said. "I'll be in touch."

They shook hands.

As he drove away, Randall looked into the rearview mirror. Kolvek was slowly shutting the side gate behind them.

In the Municipal Court
of the County of San Marin

People of the State of California,	)	D.A. No. F0877432
Plaintiff,	)	
vs.	)	Case No. _____
	)	
JOSEPH WILLIAM KOLVEK,	)	
13127 Reyna Way	)	**Complaint – Criminal** (FELONY)
Racine, California	)	
Defendant.	)	

The undersigned complains that in the County of San Marin, State of California, and before the making or filing of this Complaint, the defendant did commit the following crime(s):

COUNT ONE: On or about the month of August this year, JOSEPH WILLIAM KOLVEK did murder SHARON SUSAN KOLVEK, a human being, in violation of Penal Code section 187.

Dated: October 4, 1985

LAWRENCE HEALY,
District Attorney
County of San Marin

By: *Lawrence Healy*
    Deputy District Attorney

8

"So for those reasons, gentlemen, I believe I am compelled to deny defense counsel's motion for suppression of blood and hair samples."

Randall jumped to his feet. "But, Your Honor, in light of *United States versus Bouse*—"

Judge Davis shook his head. "Mr Randall, you've had your chance to argue your side of the case. My ruling stands. Court is adjourned."

Randall gestured to his client to stand up as the judge left the bench. Daniel Pierce was bewildered; he had been bewildered ever since he had been arrested for kidnapping over two months earlier. He leaned over to Randall and whispered, "What's going on?" Randall shushed him; the Deputy District Attorney prosecuting the case was coming over to the defense table.

"That was a tough one to lose, Jim."

Randall grunted in acknowledgement.

He knew Tom Mosher well enough to know that he was not just being friendly; he wanted to find out what Randall was going to do next. He had no intention of telling Mosher anything, even if he knew what he was going to do next, which he didn't.

The bailiff was approaching. "If you'll excuse me, Tom," Randall said, as politely as he could. When the Deputy left, he turned to his client. "Look, Dan, we can't talk here. I'll come by the jail this afternoon and explain just what happened. You have to go with the bailiff now; here he is.

The bailiff handcuffed Pierce and led him away. Randall packed up his briefcase and snapped the locks shut. He wanted to vent his anger by slamming the lid down and stomping out of the courtroom, but he didn't want Mosher to know how angry he really was. He nodded at him and walked out, refusing to comment on the ruling to the reporters in the hall. All he would say was that of course he was disappointed with the ruling.

He walked briskly the familiar route back to his office. Given the way things were going on this Friday afternoon, he was not at all surprised when a pigeon made a deposit on his briefcase on the way.

Sally was on the phone, as usual, when he came in. He rested his briefcase on her desk and waited impatiently for her to hang up. He wanted to give himself the pleasure of some indiscreet talk for a few minutes. She was saying something about booking numbers and jail cells; he was too upset to care. The moment she put the receiver down he began his tirade.

"You're not going to believe this. I still don't believe it and I was there. Judge Davis refused to suppress any of the evidence. Any of it! He gave me a bunch of bull about the samples being taken incident to arrest—what he really meant was he knew the media was right outside the door; maybe if he ruled for us he'd get some bad press and maybe he wouldn't get reelected next time. He knows damn well I'm going to appeal this and his ruling will be overturned—he wants an appeals court to take the heat so he won't have to..."

He took a deep breath. He hated a cowardly judge almost more than anything. "I'll have to discuss the options with Dan," he said in a calmer tone. "I'm going to see him later this afternoon. Call the jail, will you please, and see what time they're doing the count today. I don't want to get stuck during the lockdown."

"That should work out well for another appointment you're going to have this afternoon," Sally said.

He braced himself. "Okay," he said. "Give it to me."

She handed him her yellow notepad. "Joseph Kolvek was picked up this morning on an arrest warrant. They wouldn't give him his one call until he was booked, so he just managed to reach me about twenty minutes before you walked in."

"What! How the hell did that happen? Elizabeth told me we could surrender him at arraignment. What's she up to?"

"I called her office," Sally said. "She's out for a seminar—left yesterday morning, not due back until Sunday afternoon. I called the jail and that's the information they gave me." She nodded at the yellow pad.

Randall read out loud, "Charge is one count of murder. No other holds. Arraignment set for next Tuesday, bail set at two hundred and fifty thousand—Two hundred and fifty thousand! Where'd they get that from?"

He expected no answer and got none. He gazed out the window, thinking. "It's now three-thirty on a Friday afternoon—too late to set up a bail review hearing even if Elizabeth were here to present the D.A.'s side, which she obviously isn't. And nine'll get you ten nobody else over there is willing to make the appearance on her behalf. I could call in a favor and ask one of the judges to issue an *ex parte* bail reduction, but I don't think I have much chance of getting one—this case is too high visibility. I'm getting a little sick of having these things tried in the media."

He sighed heavily and picked up his

briefcase again. "I'd better get over to the jail now. Would you call and ask them to bring Pierce and Kolvek down for me—and could you stick around until I get back? I might need to get some paperwork done." He strode out the door without waiting for an answer.

Randall was used to the cramped, dingy interview room at the jail; he no longer noticed the windowless walls, covered with graffiti, or even the stale smell of unwashed bodies. But he automatically sat down on a legal pad rather than the bare chair seat, and kept his hands away from the underside of the table.

He had had his painful interview with Daniel Pierce and he was waiting for Joseph Kolvek. Pierce had been in no condition to listen to any careful explanation of his options; he was almost hysterical. In the end Randall had in effect to make his decision for him. He had gone through this before with clients, and he found it draining. He hoped that Kolvek was holding on to his extraordinary control even under these circumstances.

A deputy sheriff ushered Kolvek in. Randall stood up, noting that Kolvek actually looked better in prison clothes than he did in street clothes. Even the absence of a belt did not diminish him. He had a certain natural stature. And he was calm. He sat down, clasped his hands on top of the table, and waited for Randall to talk. The indignity of being booked into prison had not eroded his detachment.

Randall cleared his throat. "I know you're wondering what happened... And I'm afraid at this point I can't tell you; I don't know. There had to be some kind of slip-up in the D.A.'s office; Elizabeth Barron wouldn't go back on her word like this. She's out of the office today and she won't be back until late Sunday or early Monday, so I can't even reach her."

He explained the problem with getting an immediate reduction in bail. "So you really have only a couple of options right now. I can call a bail bondsman for you and you can pay him twenty-five thousand dollars and give him security for the balance and you'll be out tonight. But you won't get any of the twenty-five thousand back.

"Or I can try to work something out with a judge where you post a part of the bail yourself and sign over some property for the balance. As I told you before, you'd get all of that back when the case is over, but the problem with that is that it takes time and we don't have any time today before all the clerks go home.

"Your last choice, naturally, is just to stay here for the weekend. I'll get hold of Elizabeth and a judge first thing Monday morning and we'll have you O.R.ed... that means a release on your own recognizance—that's your promise to show up for the court appearances.

That's not usually granted in a case this serious, but you have unusual circumstances. You've lived here a long time, you own a business here, you're a respected community leader... I think it'll be OK. And I'm sure Elizabeth won't fight it.

"That's the one thing we've got going for us. I don't think Elizabeth meant this to happen; she's always been honest with me. So we're starting this case with her being under an obligation to us. She's going to be off balance when she hears about this. Somebody messed up over in her office, and that's to our advantage. Every little bit helps. So that's it. Of course you have the option of paying the whole two hundred fifty thousand in cash—it's all returnable to you when the case is over... unless you take off, of course."

Kolvek shook his head. "No, I don't have that kind of cash. What you're telling me is either I pay somebody twenty-five thousand dollars or I spend three nights in jail. That's it, isn't it?"

Randall sighed. "That's it, yes. I'm sorry, but you see it's the way the thing was timed. If they'd arrested you yesterday, or even this morning, and let you use the phone earlier, I would have had some room to maneuver. I'm going to try and find out whether the timing was deliberate or not, don't worry about that, but right now we just have to accept it and go from there."

Kolvek stared at his hands. "This is a dangerous place."

There was no reason to mince words with this client. "In this particular jail, we've got one thousand prisoners in a facility designed for seven hundred and seventy-five. And over the weekend it can only get worse."

He remembered, although he would of course not tell Kolvek, that a couple of years earlier in a similar jail in another county, a young man given a two day sentence for outstanding traffic tickets had been stabbed to death. In essence, he had received the death penalty for a couple of minor infractions of the law. But Kolvek had seen the conditions for himself. If he constantly looked over his shoulder, he would only be more vulnerable. Probably his natural caution and self-containment would see him through. Certainly it was not surprising that he should balk at paying twenty-five thousand dollars for two or three days of freedom.

"I'll wait until Monday," he said. "What's going to happen then?"

"Well, you're set for arraignment on Tuesday. The general rule is they have to arraign you within seventy-two hours of the arrest, which would be Monday, but of course the weekend throws the time count off. But I'm going to try to get it set for Monday morning, at the same time as a bail review. Then I'll make my pitch for an O.R., Elizabeth will have her say and the judge will decide. We'll also plead you not guilty. You'll be asked to sign a form that says you've been told your constitutional rights... By the way, did the police give you a *Miranda* warning?"

"I don't know. What's that?"

Randall wondered how Kolvek had managed to avoid seeing any police shows on television for the past fifteen years. "It's a recital of some of your rights. Your right to remain silent, and your right to have a lawyer."

"Yes, they did."

"Okay. And you haven't made any statements to anybody?"

"No. You told me not to."

"Good. If anybody should try to question you, just tell them you have an attorney and all questions should be directed to him. Don't even talk to cellmates. In cases like this they're almost always informers. Not that we're hiding anything, I don't mean to imply that, but you'd be surprised how things can get twisted. Some perfectly ordinary comment can become an admission that you're a wife beater, because that makes brownie points for the snitch with the cops. Okay. Any other questions?"

Kolvek shook his head and Randall continued. "I've put twenty dollars on the books for you, so you have a twenty-dollar credit with the jail for things like cigarettes, candy, books, and so on."

"But I had almost two hundred dollars in cash on me when they picked me up," Kolvek said mildly.

"No, that's considered part of your personal effects and it's sealed up in an envelope with your watch and the other things they took from you when you were booked. I could get it released, but it's easier to do it this way. Oh, and by the way, when they offer to let you buy cigarettes, be sure and do it."

"I don't smoke."

"I know, but it's currency. You need cigarettes to buy almost everything. Inmates run the place — trustees, and if you don't have cigarettes you could wind up eating with your fingers. Even a fork can be a luxury in here."

While they were waiting for the guard to come and release Randall, he gave Kolvek a last piece of advice. "I know I don't have to tell you just to do what you're told and not get into any arguments. Don't even be a bystander at an argument. I'll try to drop by again tomorrow. If you change your mind about the bail, call me. All the phones in here are collect, but my answering service will accept the call."

"I won't change my mind," Kolvek said flatly. Randall believed him.

The guard arrived and ushered Kolvek out. Randall, watching him go, mentally crossed his fingers, hoping that no one would read his detached, aloof manner as arrogance or, God forbid, provocation. In spite of all the guards no jail could ever be considered a controlled environment.

IN THE MUNICIPAL COURT
OF THE COUNTY OF SAN MARIN

PEOPLE OF THE STATE OF CALIFORNIA,)
) D.A. No. F0877432
                        Plaintiff,) Case No. _____
)
vs.   ) MOTION
) FOR DISCOVERY
JOSEPH WILLIAM KOLVEK,   )
                        Defendant.)
_____)

JOSEPH WILLIAM KOLVEK, defendant in the above-entitled matter, by and through his counsel, hereby moves the Court to enter an order directing that the Office of the District Attorney of the County of San Marin provide to counsel for defendant KOLVEK for inspection and, where appropriate, copying, copies of all notes, memoranda, and reports prepared in conjunction with the investigation culminating in the charges against defendant KOLVEK being filed.

This request specifically includes but is not limited to reports concerning the neighborhood canvass performed in this matter, and further includes an incident report prepared by the Police Department of Racine concerning an altercation taking place at the Sunset Bar, 456 Washington Boulevard, Racine, California, during the early morning hours of August 6, 1985

Dated: October 24, 1985   Respectfully submitted,

                                   James R. Randall

                                   JAMES R. RANDALL
                                   Attorney for Defendant

9

Jenny leaned on the doorbell for what seemed to her to be the hundredth time. She nodded to the man taking his garbage down the hall to the chute; any minute now the old lady in 22C would be taking her Pomeranian out for his walk. Jenny had been in this condominium building so often in the past ten days that she felt she knew the habits of nearly half the tenants.

There was a faint sound behind the door. Was her patience about to be rewarded? Was Mrs Simms back in town at last?

The door opened to reveal a stoutish middle-aged woman with bright blue eyes and a quantity of rouge, wearing a bright red polyester pants suit. Her very blonde hair was upswept into an amazing cluster of fat curls on the top of her head.

"Mrs Brenda Simms?" Jenny asked, surprised. She had expected a cool sophisticate.

"Oh, yes," Mrs Simms said. Her pleasant smile was encouraging.

"Mrs Simms, my name is Jenny Greyling. I'm a private investigator, and I wondered if I could have a few minutes of your time to talk about Mrs Sharon Kolvek."

The smile faded somewhat. "Well now, what about Sharon? I don't want to be rude, but after all I don't know that I want to discuss my friends with strangers."

"Oh, I understand that," Jenny said soothingly. "Of course you would feel that way. The thing is, this is rather important. It's not something I can discuss in the hallway, though..." She looked meaningfully down the hall at the door to 22C, which was opening right on schedule to emit the lady and her Pomeranian.

"Oh," Mrs Simms said. "Well, I guess..." She stood aside and Jenny preceded her into the little vestibule and then into a living room with flowered chintz upholstery and a quantity of ruffled lampshades. "What a nice apartment," Jenny said politely.

Mrs Simms gestured her into a chair and took one herself.

"Yes, I really enjoy it here. I bought it three years ago when I got divorced; I haven't regretted it for a moment." She settled back cozily. "Can I get you something? Cold drink or some coffee?"

Jenny pulled out her wallet and flipped it open to her investigator's license. "No, thanks a lot. I don't want anything, really.

Maybe you'd like to look at this to confirm I am who I say I am."

Mrs Simms waved her hand in dismissal. "No, no," she said, smiling. "I know you wouldn't lie to me; I get feelings about things like that and I'm never wrong. I trust you. But I really don't know what I can tell you about Sharon. I haven't seen her for quite a while." She leaned forward, smiling. "Now tell me the problem. Has she been naughty again?"

Jenny said gently, "I'm afraid what I'm going to say will come as a shock to you. Mrs Kolvek has been dead for some time. Her body was just found about a month ago."

"No!" The large blue eyes widened. "You don't say! That really *is* news, isn't it? How did it happen?"

Jenny was taken aback by this reaction. "We're not really certain yet," she said. "That's one of the things we're investigating. I work for an attorney, James Randall. He's representing Mrs Kolvek's husband."

"Randall. That sounds familiar." She sat back in her chair again, tapping her teeth with a red fingernail. "Randall. I know, he's that big criminal lawyer, I just saw him on TV the other day. He was talking about that messy rape case, I guess you know the one. That really sounded fascinating. Did you help him on that one? I couldn't help wondering what really happened to those poor women. The newspapers didn't give any real details."

Jenny felt as though she had fallen into a cobweb, soft and pretty, glistening with dew. A charming spot until the spider suddenly appeared. She tried to shake off the image and get down to business.

"How well did you know Mrs Kolvek, Mrs Simms? And can you tell me when you saw her for the last time?"

Mrs Simms sighed. "Oh, Sharon and I go back about three years. That's about when I got my divorce, three years ago. We met one evening in a bar. She was coming on to a fellow there; it certainly wasn't the first time, but I thought her technique was pretty crude. I took her under my wing and after a while she improved a lot. It really was a pleasure to watch her stringing them along... Of course I never had to tell her how to drop them. She had a real instinct for the knife."

Jenny hoped her face did not reveal her feelings. "Did your relationship with her develop beyond that?"

Mrs Simms gurgled — there really was no other word for it. "Honey, you certainly have a way with words. 'Relationship', I like that. It really sounds illicit!" Jenny did not respond. "Well, we did see each other quite a lot, but it wasn't planned; we just ran into each other, because we went to the same places. You see, the thing is, we didn't have anything in common. Underneath it all, she was sort of strait-laced. Really conventional. If you ask me, her one little adulterous episode put her off forever. She never dreamed of going to bed with the men she picked up; she just wanted to play games. Really, I think sometimes she disapproved of *me*, can you believe it?" She laughed lightly and shook her head. The curls, apparently frozen with hair spray, did not move.

"I see," Jenny said. "Do you remember when you saw her last?"

Mrs Simms sighed again, and looked off into space. "Let's see. I think it was back in July some time. No, come to think of it, it might have been August... I think I remember thinking it was a month without a holiday... Yes, I'm pretty sure it was August. And I think..." she wrinkled her forehead. "Yes, I'm pretty sure it was the Sunset Bar we were at. That's right, I *am* sure, because there was a big fight in the parking lot. One of Sharon's mongrels got sore and tried to bite her. Somebody called the police. It was quite a show."

"Was there a written police report?"

"Oh, sure, I think so. One of the cars got scratched or something. They took down everybody's name and address. Of course it didn't matter because none of us gave our real names. You never do at places like that. Naturally. I don't remember what name Sharon was using that night. I was calling myself 'Ellie Ramsay', I think."

"Oh, okay." Jenny was relieved to hear it. She had thought for a minute that she must have slipped up badly, because her routine check of the police records had turned up several minor brushes Mrs Kolvek had had with the law, but nothing for the night of August sixth. Nevertheless she should have checked on incidents that evening in the vicinity of the Sunset Bar. She made a note to tell Randall she would need some help in getting this particular incident report, because it would obviously not contain any of the names listed on the authorization he had given her.

Mrs Simms was still thinking. "Actually, you know, now that I come to think of it, maybe this particular guy was dumb enough to give his right name. He was some hick a cabdriver brought to the bar. He really didn't know which end was up." She laughed softly. "If you pardon my language."

"Well, exactly what happened? Do you recall the details?"

"Oh, Sharon had been onto this character all evening. You know, laughing at his jokes, drinking his booze, brushing up against him. His tongue was hanging out by the time she was ready to leave. Well, I guess I don't have to tell you about the way men are." She smiled warmly at Jenny, who forced herself to smile weakly back. "So she told him she was leaving in a special way—naturally he thought she was inviting him home with her. So she let him walk her to her car and then she let him have it. What did he think she was, who did he think *he* was... You know. Well, he took it personally, and boy, was he mad! He tried to get into her car, he called her all kinds of names. He acted like he'd known her a long time, really.

"Anyway, one thing led to another—I remember she was hitting at him with her purse and she tried to kick him. Maybe that's when the car got scratched. That's a pretty small parking lot."

"I know," Jenny said. She was somewhat surprised to learn that Sharon had had the room to swing her purse. "So somebody called the police and they came and took names and addresses but they didn't make any arrests, is that right?"

"Right, right." Mrs Simms nodded vigorously, and the curls remained static. Jenny wondered who her hairdresser was.

"Now, I've talked to the owners of the Sunset Bar, Mrs Simms. They didn't mention anything about this incident—"

"Oh, I imagine they wouldn't. I remember Joe wasn't there that night—Bob was, but I suppose he'd like to forget Sharon ever existed. He came out to the lot while all this was going on and made a couple of remarks. He said he would appreciate it if Sharon never came back to the place again. Naturally she lost her temper and she told him that she was the one who had given the bar its nasty reputation in the first place and if he wanted her to go, she'd take all his customers with her.

Listen, why don't we have a cup of tea? I'm really dying for one."

"Oh, thanks, I don't..." But Mrs Simms was already vanishing in the direction of the kitchen. Jenny decided to join her, in order not to lose both time and the thread of the inquiry.

The kitchen had frilly white curtains, delicate rose-covered wallpaper and lots of brass trivets. A ruffled apron was hanging from the handle of the refrigerator door. Mrs Simms was filling a bright red teapot. "Have a seat, honey," she said. "I think it's real cozy to have a chat in the kitchen, don't you?"

Jenny's tea came in a flowered china cup, and there were macaroons on a matching dish. "Mrs Simms," she said, after a quick sip, "did you have the feeling that Bob at the Sunset Bar really blamed Sharon for the change in his clientele?"

"Well, sure he did, he was furious, I told you. Strictly speaking, it was Sharon and I who had something to do with the clientele. When we met there the first time, we both agreed that the place was pure dullsville. Everybody was so square, you wouldn't believe it. So the next time we went Sharon did her number, and you should have seen that Bob! He acted as though she dropped a tarantula into one of his drinks. It was really funny, you couldn't help laughing. He ended up throwing Sharon out.

"So I dropped the word to some of my

friends—not the choicest friends, either. And I suppose Sharon did the same with hers. We thought we'd teach that creep a lesson, he was so narrow-minded."

"I guess your plan worked," Jenny said.

"It did, didn't it," Mrs Simms said complacently. She took another macaroon. "Maybe too well. It's getting a little bit *too* raunchy, if you ask me. Some of that sort of person might not want to take no for an answer. To tell you the truth, I haven't been going there lately. I thought that was why I haven't been seeing Sharon; I thought she was still going there." She tapped her fingernail absently against her cup. "But maybe it is time to go there again. I'm beginning to feel adventurous." She gave Jenny a dreamy smile.

"Didn't Bob recognize Sharon when she came back after he threw her out that first time?"

"Oh, no. Sharon was wearing a wig that time, a blonde one. It gave her a totally different look, and it affected her personality too. She acted different when she was wearing it . . . He's not all that bright anyway."

"Now you say Bob blamed her that night in August for the change in his place?"

"Well, she took all the credit! She made him twice as mad, saying things like that. He was really *mad*. Mad enough to kill." Their eyes met and Mrs Simms put her hand up to her mouth. "Oh, I guess I shouldn't have put it like that. You said you didn't know exactly how Sharon died. That is what you said, isn't it?"

"I said we were investigating the cause," Jenny said. "She was missing and then she was found dead, out in the country."

The blue eyes bulged a little. "Was she —" she said delicately, "did they —"

"I really can't say much about it," Jenny said. "It seems to have been a blow on the head. Just that. Nothing else." She busied herself going through her notes. There was just one more point, and then she could leave. "I notice you said something here about her one episode of adultery, or something like that. Could you explain that a little?"

"Oh, did you write all that down? You're very thorough, aren't you?"

"Well, I try to be accurate. Could you explain that a little?"

Mrs Simms got up and added hot water to her tea. "You don't want any more? How about another cookie? Well, you know, honey, I really don't think I ought to say anything about that. It was something that Sharon told me in strict confidence and it happened many, many years ago. I never discuss my friends' private lives, never."

It was obvious that the woman was not going to talk any more. She had drawn the line. Maybe she wanted to be coaxed and draw out the interview that way. She seemed to be enjoying it. Of course now she had all the information from Jenny that she was going to get about what had happened to Sharon Kolvek. Harrison Wiley, the investigator who was doing the background check in Michigan, could follow this information up.

Jenny closed her notebook and her pen and stood up. Her purse was in the living room. "Well," she said, "I really appreciate all this, Mrs Simms. You've been very generous with your time. Someone from Mr Randall's office will be contacting you if your testimony is needed."

Mrs Simms gave Jenny another of her warm smiles. "Oh, you're welcome," she said. "It's been very interesting. I'll be glad to help. You know the way out, don't you? I'm still drinking my tea."

Jenny murmured goodbye and left the apartment quickly, picking her purse up on the way. She closed the front door gently, thinking that Mrs Simms was really careless to let a total stranger walk out of her kitchen like that, without watching her leave the apartment. But that was obviously typical of Mrs Simms. She didn't seem self-destructive —just bored and looking for a little excitement. But her behavior would seem to indicate that one day she might get a little more excitement than she bargained for.

JAMES R. RANDALL
Attorney at Law
616 South Sherman Boulevard, Suite 2102
Racine, California
611/445-3123

October 15, 1985

TO WHOM IT MAY CONCERN:

The undersigned represents Joseph Kolvek in connection with a matter of significant importance. Your courtesy and cooperation in speaking with investigator Harrison Wiley would be greatly appreciated.

James R. Randall

JAMES R. RANDALL

SO AUTHORIZED:

Joseph W. Kolvek

JOSEPH W. KOLVEK

10

Harrison Wiley stopped his battered pickup truck outside the old farmhouse, and sat for a moment waiting for his insides to calm down. The road leading to the house was filled with gaping potholes and ruts; they hadn't done his stomach or his truck's shock absorbers any good.

He grunted his way out of the truck and slowly walked up the front steps. Undoubtedly he would find his subject near the back door, but he knew from years of pushing himself where he wasn't wanted that approaching the woman of the house through the kitchen door would be taken as a sign of disrespect. The porch was clean, but the condition of the paint implied that the doorbell wouldn't work. He knocked loudly three times accordingly, and then took off his hat and wiped his forehead on his sleeve. It was Indian Summer in Calhoun County, and Wiley was suffering through it like everybody else. He had been to four farms already this weekend. He reflected dolefully that if he had known what the weather was going to be like, he might not have accepted this job, although he was getting rush rates and he sure could use the money.

It was easy for Jenny Greyling out there in California. All she had to do was lift up the phone. She didn't have to drive an old pickup down a bumpy, dusty road in hundred degree heat...

The woman who stood inside the screen door looked vaguely middle-aged, and not too friendly. "Yes?" she said.

"Good morning, ma'am, my name is Harrison Wiley. I'm a licensed private investigator." He held his card out to her. "Are you Mrs Chamblin, Mrs Deborah Chamblin? Somebody told me you might be able to give me some information about a family, name of Kolvek, that used to live around here."

She hesitated and then opened the screen door and took the card.

"Well," she said, "you can come in, but I don't know as I can help you any. I haven't heard from any of them in quite a while."

Wiley followed down the hall. She had a pretty good figure and a lot of thick brown hair. She had to be somewhere in her fifties, if she was an old flame of Joseph Kolvek's. They entered a shabby living room that looked as though people really lived in it. There were a couple of magazines on a stained mahogany coffee table and some comfortable seating with plenty of old reading lamps. "Won't you take a seat?" she asked politely. "Can I get you something cold to drink?"

He did want something cold to drink, and gratefully gulped the glass of cold cider which she promptly brought him.

"That really hits the spot," he said. "Awful weather. Now I know it's getting kind of late and you'll have to be thinking about dinner pretty soon, so I just have a couple of questions and then I'll get right out of your hair. I guess you used to know Joseph Kolvek pretty well. I guess you knew the whole family before they went out west."

She looked at him dispassionately. "Just because I used to know somebody isn't a good reason to talk to a stranger about him."

He sighed and took out his wallet again. He handed her the letter from Kolvek's lawyer.

, "So," she said, handing it back after a quick reading. "Joe's got trouble."

"Yes, ma'am. And we're hoping maybe you can help him out."

"What sort of trouble?" she asked.

"Well, now, Mrs Chamblin, I'd like to discuss it, but ethically I really shouldn't. I've got to protect his interests because he's my client."

She nodded politely, and then repeated, "What sort of trouble?"

It was obvious that she was not going to cooperate without answers.

"Well," he said, "he's accused of murdering his wife."

She looked shocked and closed her eyes for a moment. He wondered whether she was seeing herself in Sharon Kolvek's coffin or, more likely, seeing Sharon Kolvek where she had often longed to put her.

He waited but she remained silent, so he said, "I understand that for a while it looked like you were going to be Mrs Joseph Kolvek. Picked out the kitchen curtains and everything."

She glared at him. "I suppose you got that from Lydia Fresham."

He had.

"Oh," she said, "don't think she's the only one around here who knows about that piece of ancient history. But she's the only one who wouldn't have the common courtesy to call me and tell me you've been nosing around."

Obviously he had stumbled on an old feud, but that was not what he was there for. "Be that as it may," he said, "and I'm not agreeing that she's the one who told me, but I guess you did know Joseph Kolvek pretty well."

"Even if I did," she snapped, "that's got nothing to do with this trouble he has now. Some things are best left alone. And I doubt

Joe would want me talking about him and me."

"Seems to me," Wiley said casually, "that maybe Joe Kolvek didn't always know just what was best for him."

She smiled slowly after a while. "You're right there," she said. Suddenly she got up and left the room.

Wiley remained seated and amused himself by finishing off the cider. The living room curtains were stirring a little in a late afternoon breeze and he felt a little better than he had when he left the truck. After about five minutes he was glad to hear her coming back; he had begun to wonder if she was just going to leave him there.

She was carrying a large photograph album. She came and sat next to him on the sofa so that he could look on with her. The cover of the album was decorated with a needlepoint daisy which had been roughly glued on. Several faded photos of a boy and girl were on the first pages—the boy was about seven, the girl maybe a little younger. They stood together, sometimes on a country road, sometimes before a small schoolhouse, sometimes in front of a gate. In one snapshot the little girl, then about nine, was laughing and bending down to take off her patent leather shoes. The boy, barefoot, was helping her keep her balance. The photograph, even though it had dimmed with age, took Wiley back to the long hot summer days of his childhood. He could almost feel the heat of the road under his bare feet and the sunlight on his hair.

"We used to walk to school together," Deborah Chamblin said. "He lived farther out then me, so he'd come by and whistle for me at the gate. I didn't see him much in the summer. His pa kept him working so he didn't get much chance to come by.

"In the winter I had dance and piano lessons sometimes after school and he had to get back and work on the farm. Well, it wasn't much of a farm—about a hundred acres of hard dirt. There was only Joe to help his pa; he didn't have any brothers or sisters. That was good because there weren't more mouths to feed, but it was hard on Joe. 'Course he built up his muscles—nobody at school dared to pick on him, or on me either, because they all knew I was Joe's girl."

Her hands kept turning the pages. Now the children were in their early teens. In one snapshot the boy was fighting a tree stump almost as tall as he was. There was a look of fierce determination on his face. The girl sat on an old stone wall watching him.

"When we were in the seventh grade Joe's pa got real sick and Joe had to miss a lot of school. Finally he just dropped out for good. My pa didn't like that, and he didn't want me to see Joe any more. I was the baby of the family; they had ambitions for me. But

I wanted Joe. So we went right on seeing each other."

She turned the pages more quickly, because most of the snapshots were of her alone. "Anyway, when the war started, Joe enlisted. His pa didn't want him to, so he enlisted under another name. He was really underage anyway. I didn't want him to do it either, but he had his mind made up and that was that. He didn't tell me where he was going or anything because he didn't want his pa to know, and sure enough when his pa kicked up a ruckus and came over to ask me questions, I really couldn't tell him anything because I didn't know anything."

She kept turning pages, rather mechanically and there were snapshots of other boys with Deborah.

"I really missed him but I never heard from him and after a while I got sore about it. I started going out with other boys. And then they found Joe and sent him home. I was awfully glad to see him, and he seemed to settle down, even though he was pretty mad at his father. But then he found out about the other boys."

She smiled at Wiley. "One thing about Joe, you know, he didn't allow for people's mistakes. I went out with other boys while he was gone, he didn't want anything more to do with me. And that was the end of it. He wouldn't even speak to me if we met in town."

She closed the book. "I don't think he knew much about women. There were plenty of girls after him, and the next thing we knew he was married to Sharon Rapinski."

Wiley cleared his throat. "I guess she was a good enough wife," he said carefully. "They were married for over thirty-five years and they had three nice kids."

She gave a short bitter laugh. "She was a slut from the word go. Everybody knew it but Joe. Joe don't let other people make mistakes, and he don't admit he made 'em either. He married her and he'd stay married to her, no matter what. He'd never back down and say he made a mistake."

"Are you saying she was unfaithful to him?"

She hesitated. "I'm saying she sure liked to flirt. You could see it here at the dances. She'd be off in corners carrying on. Men liked her too, they always did. I suppose they could tell as soon as they saw her."

"Well, lots of women like to flirt. It don't always mean anything. Some husbands even enjoy it; they want other men to be jealous of 'em."

She looked at him coldly. "I don't think Joe would get a kick out of that," she said.

"Maybe you didn't know him as well as you thought," Wiley said. "After all, people change when they grow up. You really only knew him when he was a kid."

She flushed. "Well," she said angrily, "he

might have changed, sure, but don't try to tell me he changed so much that he didn't mind raising another man's bastard!"

There was a short pause. "You mean she was pregnant when they got married?"

Her face was still red. "Well, I don't know about that," she said. "I couldn't say, not with her. But I can tell you that Joe was over in Korea in the army 'til about seven months before Tommy Kolvek was born. And we all knew who Sharon was hanging around with while Joe was gone. A fellow named Evans Jake.

"They all took off for California when Tommy was about three years old. The farm wasn't doing any better, so Joe sent money back home. About seven years ago his pa died and Joe came back for the funeral and to see to his mother."

"What about his mother?"

"Well, she didn't want to go to California," she said defensively. "Her friends were here, and Joe checked the place out real carefully, and she was really happy there for the two years she had left. She didn't want to go to California, so he found the best old people's home he could."

"Did you see him when he came back for his mother's funeral?"

She shook her head. "Joe didn't come back for that. Joe's not like that. He wouldn't have come back for his pa's funeral if he didn't have to get his mother settled. And that time he didn't even visit — he just came back and packed up and left that farm without a second look. That's Joe all over. He does what he has to do."

"Well," Wiley said, "I really appreciate your time, Mrs Chamblin. I'm going to pass all of this on to Mr Kolvek's people and I sure hope it helps him."

"That's all right," she said. "I guess Joe was in trouble from the time he first met Sharon Rapinski."

As she walked him to the door, she said, "I bet Joe'll get out of it himself. He didn't know much about women, but when he understands what's going on, there's nobody sharper than Joe. I hear he did real well for himself out there in California."

She was still clutching the photograph album.

As he bounced his way back to the main road, he noted that it looked like rain. He thought that perhaps it was the muggy heat that was making him feel rather depressed. But maybe he would feel better if he called California collect right away and unburdened himself of Deborah Chamblin's story.

DATE: October 21, 1985
MEMO TO: James Randall
FROM: Jenny Greyling
RE: Kolvek Investigation

The written report supplementing Harrison Wiley's verbal debriefing was express mailed to me, and I am attaching it herewith. I think you'll find the details very interesting.

I've done what I can to check out alibis for August 6/7, but as you know I have had very little success. My tentative findings are as follows:

Elaine Morris (daughter) -- no indication she was anywhere other than at home, but no proof to that effect. She and her husband have separate bedrooms.

Susan Jordan (daughter) -- at home all night, vouched for by husband.

Thomas Kolvek (son) -- no one saw him from the time he left the Kolvek residence until 7:45 the next morning, when he walked into the paperboy as he (Thomas) was entering his apartment building.

Joseph Kolvek (client) — phone records show he placed a long distance call from his home at 11:37 the night of the 6th.

Robert Sampson (owner/bartender) — at the Sunset Bar until it closed at 2:00 a.m. the 7th. Unable to determine whereabouts following that. Refused to speak to me when I returned to the bar for additional information.

Wilbur ("Joe") Thompson (owner/bartender) -- did not work that night. No recollection of what he did, but no evidence of any contact with Sharon Kolvek.

Brenda Simms (friend) — as shown by incident report, at Sunset Bar until at least 0143 hours August 7 under name of Ellie Ramsey. No proof of whereabouts after altercation.

11

Randall tossed the packet of reports across his desk to Sally. "What do you make of that?"

"What makes you think I've read them?" she asked. "They're marked 'Personal and Confidential'."

He laughed. "Even if the envelope was sealed in blood and marked 'For the private attention of James Randall Only', we both know you'd still open it and read it when it came in."

"Oh," she said, "especially if it were sealed in blood. You know, I think the reason you have me open all the mail isn't because you have such great trust in me. I think it's because you want me to get the letter bombs, not you."

She laughed but Randall wasn't amused.

"That's not funny," he said. "If you think anything looks suspicious or peculiar, I don't want you opening it, you understand?"

"Hey, I was only kidding. I'm careful."

"Yeah, well, it's no joke. The Pierce trial is coming up; crackpots are going to be coming out of the woodwork all over the place."

"They're coming out already," Sally said. "I got three phone calls today and yesterday about kidnappers getting the electric chair. And their lawyers too."

"Don't waste your time talking to them," Randall said. "Now I want to get the Kolvek thing moving in the right direction before I get caught up with Pierce. So now what do you think of these reports?"

Sally picked them up and flicked through them. She had already read them.

"Well," she said thoughtfully, "I guess the Wiley report is the most interesting. If you accept the idea that Thomas Kolvek is not Joseph's son."

"If you do accept that — and all we have is the word of a woman who obviously hates Sharon Kolvek's guts, I'm aware of that — but anyway if you accept it just for the kind of light it would shed on things if it were true — you can't help noticing that Thomas isn't the kind of guy who seems to be able to do anything on his own. *And* he wanted his father to give him money. And then we find a reference to Sharon's saying on that night of August sixth something about Thomas being his father's son. Could that possibly have been a kind of subtle threat that she would tell Joseph the truth?"

"That would certainly have been the end

of Thomas," Sally said dryly, "given what we have heard about Joseph's disposition. He isn't exactly crazy about Thomas as it is."

"Yes, you could only call a threat like that a good motive for murder. Assuming it was a threat. Assuming Kolvek doesn't know about Thomas. Assuming Thomas really *isn't* his son. And assuming, of course, that Thomas knows he isn't. A lot of assumptions."

Sally went to the door. "Let me just give the calls to the answering service," she said.

When she came back she settled cozily into her chair.

"Okay," she said. "We've got a scenario with Thomas Kolvek as the murderer. With about a million assumptions."

"All right," Randall said. He put his feet up on the desk and leaned back in his chair. "Thomas is all wound up to ask his father — or the man who thinks he's his father — for a loan. One more time. He sees his mother acting up all evening, putting Joseph in an unreceptive mood. But he gives it a shot anyway. Naturally Kolvek turns him down, and then Sharon laughs at him and drops some hints about his not being Kolvek's son. If Kolvek knew that, not only would he never get a loan, but he'd lose his job and any chance of an inheritance from Kolvek. Right?

"So Thomas leaves as soon as he can and we presume he goes home. A few hours later Sharon phones him and says she wants to get away from Kolvek for a while and go up to the cabin. She's done it before, and she asks Thomas to drive her there because she's afraid to drive on those roads herself.

"So we've got Thomas going back to the Kolvek house—no, wait, his car hasn't got a muffler, and anyway I don't like the idea of it's being parked in the driveway all night. No, let's say Sharon drives over to his place and they go on from there. It takes about an hour to drive to the cabin. They get into an argument—not too hard to imagine. And Thomas stops the car. Let's say he's so mad he can't see straight."

"Or maybe they stop because she's feeling the drinks she had at the Sunset Bar," Sally said. "She sounds like the kind of woman who would rather pull over than wait another ten minutes to get to a bathroom."

"That's good," Randall said. "Anyway, they stop and get out of the car. Maybe they walk a little way into the woods. Sharon says one word too many and Thomas picks up a rock and beans her with it. Then he panics. He leaves her there and runs back to the car and drives a little way up the road. Then he realizes he can't drive her car all the way back home. So he shoves it into some bushes and trees to hide it and then he walks to the nearest bus station and goes home."

"Not too bad," Sally said judiciously. "But there are a few holes in it. For one thing, there's the rock. Would he carry it on the bus with him? They didn't find it anywhere near the body."

"Okay. Maybe he tossed it pretty far away. Or maybe it was lying there and the blood was washed off it and erosion changed its contours."

"Oh, come on!" Sally said. "Tossing it a good distance away, yes, possible. But in six weeks even a soft rock wouldn't change its contours."

Randall shrugged. "Okay, scratch the erosion. What else is wrong?"

"Well, the timing. It's pretty tight. Jenny says Thomas was seen the next morning at quarter to eight, and we know that Sharon was at the Sunset Bar until at least two a.m. Right?"

Randall picked up Jenny's memo and scanned it quickly.

"So," Sally went on, "she's got to get home after two a.m., pack her bags, pick up Thomas and drive out to the cabin with him. He's got to kill her, hide the car and get home somehow. It's all supposed to happen within five hours. I can't see it."

"Well, it's not impossible," Randall said.

"That's true. But then we come to my biggest objection. We have to assume that one, Thomas knows Joseph is not his father, and two, Joseph does not know."

Randall thought about Thomas's horrified reaction to what had seemed to be an innocent remark about there being only one

Kolvek in the room. "I think that Thomas did know," he said, "given his behavior. And as far as Joseph is concerned, we've been told over and over again that Joseph has a talent for not seeing what he doesn't want to see."

Sally thought and then shook her head. "I don't know about that. It strikes me that Joseph sees everything, but he doesn't admit to it unless he knows it's to his advantage to do it. But I agree with you that he probably wouldn't have kept Thomas on if he thought Thomas wasn't his son."

"Thomas had a further motive," Randall said. "Sharon Kolvek left everything to her son. I'll bet you anything Thomas didn't know about the division of the community property. Even if he did, Sharon's cash settlement isn't peanuts."

They both sat in silence for a moment.

"Well," Randall said, "do you have any pet ideas of your own?"

Sally nodded. "Well, I do. Do you remember the name of that man who got into the altercation with Sharon in the parking lot of the bar?"

Randall leaned over to riffle through the papers on his desk. "No, not offhand," he said. "I haven't got a photographic memory." He pulled one paper out. "Ah, here it is. Sharon Rapinski — she used her maiden name — Evans Jake, and Ellie Ramsay — that's Mrs Simms." He paused. "The guy's name was Evans Jake. Why does that sound familiar?"

Sally smiled. "Wiley's report."

Randall looked at her uncomprehendingly.

"Sharon's boy friend back in Michigan," Sally said. "The one who everyone there thinks is Thomas's father."

Randall stared at her, examining the implications of this new information. "What a can of worms," he said slowly. "It's an awfully odd name to be a coincidence. No wonder Simms said the guy seemed to take the brushoff personally."

"You'd think Sharon would have left as soon as she spotted him," Sally said. "Or at least go some place with him where they could talk privately."

"It had been over thirty years," Randall said. "Maybe she didn't recognize him."

"If Sharon told Thomas she had seen his real father that night —" Sally said. She left the sentence unfinished. "But if we forget about Thomas, let's say Evans Jake follows her home. Maybe he hasn't got anything special in mind. And let's say she doesn't notice he's following her and she decides to go up to the cabin. Maybe she calls Thomas to drive her, and he doesn't answer his phone for some reason. So she decides she wants to go badly enough to drive herself.

"So he follows her. Then she stops the car, for whatever reason, and since he doesn't know exactly where she's headed, he takes this chance to confront her. He pulls up behind her, gets out of his car, they have a confrontation and the same scenario goes that we applied to Thomas. Except here, of course, he's got his own car so he can get away afterward without any trouble. He just drives away. What do you think of that?"

"Not half bad," Randall said. "Really not half bad. Once we find him we'll have Jenny find out what time he got to wherever he was going when he left the bar. A definite possibility. Assuming of course it's the same Evans Jake. It's an odd name, but it could happen."

He thought for a while longer and then bestirred himself. "Any other suspects?"

She shook her head. "I don't have any. But Jenny sort of likes the black widow."

"The who?"

Sally laughed. "Brenda Simms. Jenny says she's like a black widow spider. She says she thinks she could have killed Sharon just for kicks. I'm sure she's not really serious about it, but the woman really freaked her out. What about you? You have any other ideas?"

"Let's keep the bartender in the back of our minds. Don't forget he found out that night that Sharon had wrecked all his plans for his bar. He's not exactly rational on the subject, is he? I mean, that's the impression I got from the report. He practically foams at the mouth when he thinks about what happened to the Sunset. We could substitute him for the killer and use the same script you provided for Evans Jake."

Sally nodded. Then she laughed. "Talk about convicting people on circumstantial evidence! Listen to us!"

"Listen, we don't need much evidence," Randall said. All we have to do is demonstrate that Joseph Kolvek is not the only person who could have murdered his wife.

"And you know, there are some other people we haven't even mentioned. For instance how about that daughter, Elaine. She had a weird relationship with her mother. Always trying to change her, to fit her into a more acceptable mould. We only have her word for it that she didn't hear from her mother after that dinner party. We have to remember that we don't know for sure that the murder occurred on the sixth or the seventh. Sharon Kolvek could have called her from the cabin and asked her to come up. Maybe they had a quarrel. Sharon seems to have had a knack for driving people berserk."

"But Sharon couldn't have called from the cabin," Sally said. "No phone."

Randall brushed that off. "Well, whatever. You can find phones. Anyway, we'd better get a move on. We've got other clients besides Kolvek. And Pierce."

Sally remained sitting. "I did have one question. I don't understand how Kolvek got the money to start up a major construction business from just selling his father's farm. In these reports it says it was just a hundred acres of dirt."

"Yes," Randall said slowly. "That struck me too. Except that I got some more background from Bill Eden. It seems that Kolvek's father started out back in the twenties with two hundred acres. Barely self-supporting for a farm in the East. Then the government started whittling away at it—a little bit for utility wires, a little bit more for sewer lines and a big chunk here and there for roads out to the subdivisions.

"So by the time Joseph inherited it he was advised to sell it—He had an offer that covered the back taxes and a little bit more. But he didn't take the advice. He hung onto it. He just let it sit there, and I gather everyone thought he was a stubborn jackass for doing it. But all those snippets taken out of it—it had good access to the major freeways and easy hookup to utilities and water and sewers. So a developer came along and thought it was a great place to put a shopping mall and a housing subdivision."

"But I thought Michigan was in the middle of a big recession five years ago," Sally said.

Randall smiled. "That's true of parts of Michigan. Detroit isn't the only city in the state, you know. And cars aren't the only industry. Kolvek's land was right near Battle Creek. The home of the Kellogg Company."

"Oho!"

"Exactly. People are going to eat breakfast cereal no matter what happens to the economy. And of course Kellogg is into other things. They employ a lot of people, those people need a place to live and they have to buy things. So Joseph Kolvek got the last laugh."

"If he ever laughs," Sally said.

"Oh, I don't know. I think almost a million dollars is enough to draw a little chuckle out of Joseph Kolvek. Okay. Now let's get a couple things out of the way. Would you draft a rough response to this letter from Carl Mersham? Tell him that, so far as I know, it is not a valid defense to a charge of assault to say that your girlfriend keeps putting onions in your tunafish salad sandwiches."

Stephanie F. Shallot

CERTIFIED GRAPHOLOGIST

SIGNATURE COMPARISON

Evidence Submitted:

Ex. 1 : Handwriting exemplar represented to be that of JOSEPH WILLIAM KOLVEK.

Ex. 2 : Certified copy of driver's license bearing signature known to be that of SHARON KOLVEK.

Ex. 3 : Three (3) charge slips, dated August 10, August 11, and August 25, 1985, bearing signatures purporting to be those of SHARON KOLVEK.

Conclusions:

Neither the writer of Ex. 1 nor the writer of Ex. 2 appear to be responsible for the questioned signatures appearing on Ex. 3. Numerous unexplained variations or differences are noted between the handwritings in Exhibits 1 and 2 and that appearing on Ex. 3. All three signatures appearing on Ex. 3 are concluded to have been made by the same hand.

12

An image floated in Randall's brain of the Hershey bar hidden in the middle drawer of his desk. He thought he might have time to eat it before Sally came back from lunch. He had just put his hand in the drawer when quick footsteps sounded in the outer office; a second later Sally opened the door and poked her head in.

"I just came back to tell you that — " she broke off as Randall swiftly took his hand out of the drawer and slammed it shut. She looked at him with her eyes narrowed. Sally and Kay had conspired to make him lose ten pounds by Christmas, and a little thing like his lack of cooperation wasn't going to stop them. He thought sadly that his candy bar was not going to survive his next absence from the office.

Sally evidently did not intend to make an issue out of it; she opened her mouth to continue, but was interrupted by the sound of the outer door. She leaned back to see who it was, and then leaned in again. "The reason I came back early was to let you know that Mr Kolvek had to move up his appointment. He's here now, and somebody's with him."

Kolvek stood up when Randall came into the outer office. There was indeed someone with him. A very elegant woman. The beautifully tailored grey suit, the well-made black leather bag and shoes, the carefully coiffed graying hair which obviously disdained a touch-up... she obviously had a quiet confidence which did not require flashy accessories. A pearl, Randall thought, not a rhinestone.

"Randall, this is Margaret Walters," Kolvek said.

She remained seated, and extended her hand and smiled at Randall, who took the hand briefly and returned the smile.

"Margaret's a friend of mine," Kolvek said. "She thought she might be able to give you some ideas about this case."

"Of course," Randall said. "I'll be happy to listen to anything you might want to tell me, Ms Walters. Did you both want to come in together, or would you prefer I speak to Ms Walters alone?"

She and Kolvek exchanged glances. She rose gracefully from her chair. "I think perhaps it will be easier for everybody if I talk to Mr Randall alone, Joseph." Kolvek nodded.

Once seated inside Randall's office with the door closed, she came directly to the point. "I think you should know right away, Mr Randall, that I am Joseph's fiancee."

Randall had not thought that Joseph Kolvek could offer him any further surprises. "Oh," he said carefully.

She smiled. "I can see that you're surprised. Perhaps you don't quite realize that Joseph Kolvek is a very attractive man. He is stable, he has a bedrock steadiness... He has unusual qualities. And no woman in her right mind would give him up lightly."

Randall thought of Deborah Chamblin and her album of memories. "I know what you mean," he said.

She leaned forward, resting her hand lightly on his desk. "I hope you do, Mr Randall. I intend to stand by Joseph all the way in this matter. And I want you to know that. I also want you to understand that before Sharon's death there was nothing between Joseph and me. And that was not by my choice. It was by Joseph's choice."

She looked into his eyes for a moment, and then sat back and continued.

"We met after a contractors' association meeting. I'm a widow, my husband was also a contractor and I maintain my ties with his world. I went to the meeting to pick up a friend, and Joseph came out with him, that's how we met. The three of us went to my house for a cup of coffee... Joseph and I met several times after that, at 'spontaneous' meetings which I carefully arranged."

She laughed. "I must admit being the aggressor was a new experience for me. And Joseph did not make it easy. He seemed completely oblivious to my motives. Then one day he told me rather abruptly that he was married. I knew that, of course. And he said he did not believe in divorce. That was all he said. That was all he ever said, even after Sharon disappeared. He does not air his grievances. Even now."

Randall nodded again. That was consistent with what he knew of Kolvek.

"But I met Sharon at a banquet one evening. She really wasn't the sort of wife Joseph needed, Mr Randall, I won't mince words about that. She wasn't sophisticated, she couldn't help Joseph acquire the polish he needs, because he's really going to be a community leader. I think I've already been able to help him a little ..."

That explained the changes in interior decoration in Kolvek's house.

She frowned. "But really no one could have taught anything to Sharon Kolvek. She just wasn't interested in learning. I saw at once when I met her that she would have pulled Joseph down instead of helping him. She was an unfortunate kind of wife for him."

She paused for a moment, brooding, and then her face cleared.

"But that's all over now. I really think I can help Joseph achieve his true potential. Even he doesn't know how far he can go." She leaned forward again, intently, and put her hand back on Randall's desk. "So you can see how important it is for us to get this matter cleared up, to put it behind us. Joseph has been stagnating for years. Now he can move rapidly ahead. Just as soon as all of this is behind him."

She paused and looked into Randall's eyes. "I want to impress on you that I am more than willing to do anything I can to help Joseph. Just tell me what it is and I will do it."

Randall felt that there was more to that statement than an indication of simple support. He felt, too, that it would not be in his client's best legal interests for him to know what that something more was. But he was curious about a different matter.

"Mrs Walters, could you tell me why you have only now decided to come and talk to me? This case has been pending for almost two months now."

She nodded and opened her handbag. "Yes, I don't blame you for wondering. Joseph wouldn't let me come before this. He said I had nothing to do with this case and he didn't want me to become involved with it. But then I received this." She took out a folded piece of paper and handed it to Randall.

He recognized it immediately. It was a subpoena from Elizabeth Barron for Margaret Walters' appearance at the preliminary hearing. He put it down on the blotter and tapped it absently with his finger. "So the prosecution wants you to testify at the prelim. Has any investigator tried to talk to you yet?"

She nodded. "Yes, two days ago, when this was served. I refused to talk to him, and he left his card." She handed it to him and he looked at it and gave it back. He didn't see any reason to add to his collection of Bud Janis's cards.

"I wanted to talk to you before I talked to anybody else," she said. "Do you think I should talk to them? Should I tell them I know Joseph couldn't possibly have committed a crime like this?"

Randall fidgeted with his pencil for a moment. "I cannot and will not tell you not to talk to the D.A.," he said. "That would be obstructing their access to a witness. But I can tell you that I can't see any way that your talking to them would help Mr Kolvek and I can think of several ways in which it could damage him. But it's your decision."

"I understand," she said.

"I have one last question for you," Randall said. "Do you know how they got your name as a possible witness?"

"Yes, I'm afraid they found it in Joseph's address book. They took it when they searched Joseph's house right after he was arrested."

Randall remembered asking Kolvek if his address book contained any names that might be personally embarrassing to him, and he remembered Kolvek saying that it did not. He told this to Margaret Walters.

"I suppose he didn't even remember it was in there," she said. "He certainly knows my phone number by heart now; he doesn't have to look it up. And I suppose he hasn't got a lot of personal phone numbers in that book."

Randall nodded absently, flipping his pencil through his fingers.

"Well, I don't think this is going to present too much of a problem. I think the deputy D.A. is taking a shot in the dark by calling you to the stand, so I don't imagine she'll ask you a lot of questions. Lawyers hate that, you know, asking questions when they don't already know the answers. So don't worry about it." He smiled at her and pushed his chair back. She rose again in her graceful way.

"Well, I do appreciate your taking the time to talk with me. Shall I send Joseph in now?"

He stood in the doorway and watched her bend over and murmur to Kolvek who rose at once. She settled down with a magazine. Sally caught his eye and handed him a document. "It's the graphologist's report," she said in a low voice. "Just came in."

Randall skimmed it as he followed Kolvek into his office. Somebody had forged Sharon Kolvek's name on these charge slips, but it hadn't been Joseph Kolvek. One less thing to worry about.

"I don't think Mrs Walters will have a bad time at the preliminary hearing," he said. "She might not even be called; they haven't got anything specific to ask her."

"She doesn't have anything to do with this," Kolvek said. "I don't want her bothered."

"Don't worry," Randall said. He leaned back in his swivel chair and took up his pencil again. "I don't think anyone will bother her. But I'm glad you brought her in; glad to meet her. Now the main reason I wanted to see you today was to let you know what you could expect at the preliminary hearing. It starts next Monday, and I think it will take two days. There will be a judge, no jury. The prosecution will put on some of its evidence—not all of it, just enough to convince the judge that they have reasonable grounds to mount a trial against you.

"Now we have the option of either putting on a full-fledged defense to try and end the case now, or of putting on almost no defense and using the prelim to find out how strong the prosecution's case is. In this case I don't see how a full-fledged defense is going to help. They can show that you had the opportunity and the ability to kill your wife, and we don't have any solid evidence that you didn't do it. Even if we gave away everything we have at this point the judge would probably just say that there's no definitive proof one way or the other and the jury will have to decide. So I think we'd better use the prelim to learn what we can about the prosecution's case. Either way is going to end up with a bindover."

Kolvek looked at him.

"A bindover occurs when a Municipal Court judge says there's sufficient evidence to hold the defendant to answer," Randall explained, "and the case goes to the Superior Court for trial. It doesn't mean the judge has decided you're guilty; it just means that he thinks there's reason to think you might be guilty, so there's reason for the state to proceed to trial."

"So this hearing won't be the end of it," Kolvek said.

"Probably not. At this hearing we'll try to find out everything the prosecution has against you — or at least everything they're willing to let us know about. I don't think they have much that we don't know about already. We've already had a motion for discovery, and we've gotten all their reports.

"We should also be able to use the hearing to get some information from people who haven't been willing to talk to us before. I'm thinking particularly of the man who was involved with your wife in an altercation on the night of the sixth. Evans Jake." He looked at Kolvek, who continued to stare at him impassively. If he recognized the name, he didn't react.

"We'll try to find out what he knows.

We've started to look into him, but he's not cooperating. We do know that he didn't report back to his office on Wednesday morning, the seventh, and he was expected to. But basically we're in the same position with him as Elizabeth Barron is with Mrs Walters; we'll be asking questions in the dark. It's not a good idea, but in this case I think it's the only way I'm ever going to find out what he knows. He has to answer my questions when he's on the stand unless the prosecution claims it's irrelevant and the judge agrees. But I don't think that'll happen. In fact I think Elizabeth will be just as interested in everything that happened that night as we are. Are you with me so far?"

Kolvek nodded. "Will I be saying anything at this hearing?"

Randall shook his head emphatically. "Definitely not. I might not even put you on the stand at the trial, although we don't have to think about that yet. But certainly I'm not going to give Elizabeth Barron the chance to get hold of you at this point."

"All right," Kolvek said.

Randall brought his chair around and put hs feet on the floor. "There's just one more thing I'd like to discuss with you. As you know, you're charged with one count first degree murder."

He picked up his unannotated Penal Code and flipped through the pages. "First degree murder, it says here, is 'All murder which is perpetrated by means of a destructive device or explosive, knowing use of ammunition designed primarily to penetrate metal or armor, poison, lying in wait, torture, or any other kind of wilful, deliberate and premeditated killing.' Plus any murder done in the commission of felonies, which doesn't apply here. What does apply here are the words 'wilful, deliberate and premeditated.' The prosecution is going to allege that you decided in advance that you were going to kill your wife, that you planned the killing and that you did it. Now second degree murder removes the element of premeditation and consequently carries a lesser penalty.

"The reason I'm telling you this is that the D.A.'s office has made us an offer. If you'll plead to second degree, they'll drop the first degree charge. They won't make any commitment about the sort of time they'll ask for. Are you interested?"

Kolvek hesitated. "I don't understand. Are you telling me I should plead guilty?"

"Absolutely not," Randall said vehemently. "I didn't say that at all. But it's my duty as your lawyer to present all your options to you. It's your decision if you want to accept any of them. This offer just came in yesterday, and I have to tell you about it.

"At the moment the evidence against you is not stronger than the evidence against a number of other people. As far as I'm concerned, the D.A. had no business filing against you with what they have. But we'll have a better idea of where we stand after the prelim — of course there's always the chance that the prosecution will feel more secure after a bindover and won't renew the offer. But it has to be up to you. Now do you want me to tell Elizabeth Barron that we accept her offer?"

"Absolutely not." Kolvek spoke unhesitatingly. His uncharacteristic use of an extra word told Randall how strongly he felt.

"Okay," Randall said. "That's all I wanted to know. Meet me here on Monday morning about eight-thirty and we'll walk over to the courthouse together."

TRANSCRIPT OF PRELIMINARY HEARING

PEOPLE OF THE STATE OF CALIFORNIA

vs. JOSEPH WILLIAM KOLVEK

COUNTY OF SAN MARIN, STATE OF CALIFORNIA

Monday, November 11, 1985 — Afternoon Session: 1:30 p.m.

THE COURT: WELL, COUNSEL, I HOPE YOU BOTH HAD A NICE LUNCH. I KNOW I DID.

LET'S SEE, WE LEFT OFF AT THE END OF INVESTIGATOR JANIS' DIRECT EXAMINATION. MS. BARRON, DO YOU HAVE ANY FURTHER QUESTIONS ON DIRECT?

MS. BARRON: NO, YOUR HONOR.

THE COURT: MR. RANDALL, ANY QUESTIONS ON CROSS-EXAMINATION?

MR. RANDALL: JUST A COUPLE, YOUR HONOR, IF I MAY.

THE COURT: FINE. CLERK, RECALL THE WITNESS, PLEASE.

HENRY JANIS,

HAVING PREVIOUSLY BEEN CALLED AS A WITNESS BY AND

ON BEHALF OF THE PEOPLE, AND HAVING PREVIOUSLY BEEN SWORN, WAS EXAMINED AND TESTIFIED AS FOLLOWS:

THE COURT: HAVING DONE THIS FOR SO MANY YEARS, MR. JANIS, I'M SURE YOU'RE AWARE THAT YOU'RE STILL UNDER OATH FROM YOUR TESTIMONY THIS MORNING.

THE WITNESS: YES, YOUR HONOR.

THE COURT: FINE. PLEASE PROCEED, MR. RANDALL.

MR. RANDALL: THANK YOU, YOUR HONOR.

NOW, MR. JANIS, ON DIRECT THIS MORNING YOU TESTIFIED THAT YOU PERSONALLY WENT TO THE SUNSET BAR TO ASCERTAIN MRS. KOLVEK'S WHEREABOUTS THE NIGHT OF AUGUST 6, 1985, IS THAT CORRECT?

THE WITNESS: THE LATE NIGHT HOURS OF AUGUST 6, EARLY MORNING HOURS OF AUGUST 7, YES.

Q: THANK YOU. AND WERE YOU ABLE TO GET AN ANSWER TO YOUR QUESTIONS?

A: YES. USING A POLICE REPORT PROVIDED TO US BY YOUR OFFICE AND USING A PHOTOGRAPH OF THE DECEASED, WE WERE ABLE TO FIND SEVERAL PEOPLE WHO REMEMBERED MRS. KOLVEK HAD BEEN IN THE BAR THE NIGHT OF THE 6TH, THOUGH SHE HAD BEEN USING A DIFFERENT NAME, AND IDENTIFIED HER AS THE

INDIVIDUAL INVOLVED IN THE ALTERCATION THAT EVENING, OR RATHER EARLY THE MORNING OF THE 7TH, AT APPROXIMATELY 1:45 A.M.

Q: AND YOU PERSONALLY CANVASSED THE NEIGHBORHOOD AROUND THE KOLVEK HOUSE TO SEE IF ANYONE HAD SEEN SHARON KOLVEK AT ANY TIME AFTER 1:45 THE MORNING OF THE 7TH?

A: YES.

Q: AND HAD ANYONE?

A: NO ONE IN THE NEIGHBORHOOD COULD RECALL HAVING SPECIFICALLY SEEN MRS. KOLVEK AT ANY TIME AFTER 9:30 THE EVENING OF THE 6TH, BUT THERE WAS A WOMAN WHO SAID SHE SAW AN UNIDENTIFIED INDIVIDUAL —

MR. RANDALL: OBJECTION. NO FOUNDATION. OUTSIDE THE SCOPE OF THE QUESTION.

THE COURT: MR. RANDALL, ARE YOU OBJECTING TO YOUR OWN QUESTION?

MR. RANDALL: YOUR HONOR, I'M OBJECTING TO THE ANSWER, NOT THE QUESTION. FIRST, NO FOUNDATION HAS BEEN LAID CONCERNING THE ALLEGED INTERVIEW, AND SECOND, THE ANSWER DOESN'T FOLLOW THE BEST EVIDENCE RULE.

THE COURT: WELL, NOW, YOU'VE ALREADY LET THE

WITNESS TESTIFY IN VAGUE TERMS ABOUT WHAT HE HEARD AT THE SUNSET BAR WITHOUT OBJECTION.

MR. RANDALL: THIS IS SOMEWHAT DIFFERENT, YOUR HONOR. THE WITNESS IS ATTEMPTING TO GO OUTSIDE THE SCOPE OF MY QUESTION.

MS. BARRON: YOUR HONOR, THE PEOPLE WILL BE CALLING THE OTHER WITNESS. WE HAVE NO OBJECTION TO THE LATTER PART OF MR. JANIS' ANSWER BEING STRICKEN.

THE COURT: THE OBJECTION IS SUSTAINED. IF THE PEOPLE HAVE A SPECIFIC WITNESS WHO OBSERVED AN INCIDENT, THE COURT AGREES WITH MR. RANDALL THAT WITNESS SHOULD TESTIFY TO IT.

PROCEED, MR. RANDALL.

MR. RANDALL: SO AS FAR AS YOU KNOW FOR SURE, MRS. KOLVEK NEVER RETURNED TO HER HOME AFTER LEAVING IT AT APPROXIMATELY 9:30 THE EVENING OF AUGUST 6, IS THAT CORRECT?

THE WITNESS: WELL, NOT SPECIFICALLY, BUT WE CAN ASSUME SHE DID BECAUSE MR. KOLVEK TOLD THE MISSING PERSONS OFFICER THAT CLOTHES HAD BEEN —

THE COURT: MR. JANIS, YOU KNOW BETTER THAN THAT. YOU CAN'T TESTIFY TO WHAT WAS TOLD ANOTHER INVESTIGATING OFFICER. ADDITIONALLY, COUNSEL

DIDN'T ASK FOR ASSUMPTIONS, HE ASKED WHAT YOU KNOW. I DON'T KNOW WHAT YOU'RE TRYING TO DO, BUT I WON'T TOLERATE IT. CONFINE YOUR ANSWERS TO THE QUESTIONS, PLEASE.

MR. RANDALL, PROCEED.

MR. RANDALL: NO FURTHER QUESTIONS AT THIS TIME, YOUR HONOR.

THE COURT: MS. BARRON?

MS. BARRON: NOTHING FURTHER, YOUR HONOR.

THE COURT: YOU'RE EXCUSED FOR THE PRESENT, MR. JANIS.

MS. BARRON: WE ASK THAT CECILIA MAYRICK BE CALLED.

CECILIA MAYRICK,
HAVING BEEN CALLED AS A WITNESS BY AND ON BEHALF OF THE PEOPLE, AND HAVING BEEN DULY SWORN, WAS EXAMINED AND TESTIFIED AS FOLLOWS:

MS. BARRON: DR. MAYRICK, BY WHOM ARE YOU EMPLOYED?

THE WITNESS: THE COUNTY OF SAN MARIN.

Q: IN WHAT CAPACITY?

A: I WORK IN THE CORONER'S OFFICE, AS A PATHOLOGIST.

Q: AND HOW LONG HAVE YOU WORKED IN THAT CAPACITY?

A: FOR THE COUNTY OF SAN MARIN, FOR THREE YEARS. BEFORE THAT I WAS EMPLOYED IN THE SAME CAPACITY BY THE COUNTY OF MAIDA.

Q: WHAT ARE YOUR QUALIFICATIONS FOR THIS POSITION?

A: I RECEIVED MY DEGREE AS A DOCTOR OF MEDICINE FROM THE UNIVERSITY OF CALIFORNIA, LOS ANGELES, AND SUBSEQUENTLY PERFORMED MY RESIDENCY AT THE —

MR. RANDALL: FOR THE PURPOSES OF THIS HEARING, YOUR HONOR, THE DEFENSE WILL STIPULATE TO THE WITNESS'S QUALIFICATIONS.

THE COURT: THE RECORD WILL INDICATE IT HAS BEEN SO STIPULATED.

MS. BARRON: THANK YOU.

DO YOU RECALL ON SEPTEMBER 17 OF THIS YEAR PERFORMING AN AUTOPSY ON ONE SHARON KOLVEK?

THE WITNESS: I DO.

Q: WHAT WERE THE CIRCUMSTANCES UNDER WHICH THE BODY WAS BROUGHT TO YOU?

MR. RANDALL: OBJECTION —

THE WITNESS: I DON'T KNOW. THAT'S AN ADMINISTRATIVE FUNCTION AND I DON'T HAVE ANYTHING TO DO WITH THAT.

THE COURT: WELL, THE WITNESS SEEMS TO HAVE TAKEN CARE OF YOUR OBJECTION FOR ME, MR. RANDALL.

GO AHEAD, MS. BARRON.

MS. BARRON: BUT IN ANY EVENT, ON SEPTEMBER 17 YOU PERFORMED THE AUTOPSY, IS THAT CORRECT?

THE WITNESS: THAT'S RIGHT.

Q: DID YOU PERFORM THE AUTOPSY ALONE?

A: NO, MY ASSISTANT, DR. MICHAEL PEARCE, WAS WITH ME.

Q: CAN YOU TELL ME BRIEFLY WHAT THE AUTOPSY DISCLOSED?

A: IT IS ALL RIGHT IF I LOOK AT MY NOTES?

Q: CERTAINLY.

THE COURT: LET THE RECORD SHOW THAT WITNESS REFERRED TO WRITTEN NOTES WHILE TESTIFYING.

THE WITNESS: WELL, BRIEFLY, THE BODY WAS THAT OF A MIDDLE-AGED CAUCASIAN FEMALE AND WAS IN VERY POOR CONDITION. IT HAD APPARENTLY BEEN EXPOSED TO THE ELEMENTS FOR QUITE SOME TIME AND

WAS IN A STATE OF SEVERE DECOMPOSITION AND SOME AREAS WERE EXTENSIVELY MAGGOT-INFESTED.

BECAUSE OF THE CONDITION OF THE BODY WE WERE NOT ABLE TO DO A COMPLETE AUTOPSY, BUT SO FAR AS WE WERE ABLE TO DETERMINE, DEATH WAS CAUSED BY BLEEDING INTO THE CRANIUM AND SUBSEQUENT PRESSURE ON THE BRAIN, DUE TO A BLOW ON THE HEAD.

MS. BARRON: WHAT SORT OF BLOW TO THE HEAD?

A: A BLOW DELIVERED BY A BLUNT INSTRUMENT AT AN OBLIQUE ANGLE FROM ABOVE. FRAGMENTS OF A ROCK OF SEDIMENTARY NATURE —

MR. RANDALL: OBJECTION.

THE COURT: SUSTAINED. UNLESS YOU'RE ALSO A GEOLOGIST, DR. MAYRICK, I'M AFRAID YOU CAN'T TESTIFY TO THE NATURE OF THE ROCK.

THE WITNESS: I'M SORRY.

MS. BARRON: BUT YOU DO BELIEVE THE INSTRUMENT USED TO DELIVER THE BLOW WAS A ROCK?

A: WE REMOVED FRAGMENTS OF ROCK FROM THE VICINITY OF THE FRACTURE SITE.

THE COURT: MS. BARRON, DO YOU INTEND TO PRESENT TESTIMONY AS TO THE EXACT NATURE OF THIS ROCK?

MS. BARRON: NO, YOUR HONOR, I DON'T CONSIDER THAT AN ISSUE IN THIS CASE.

THE COURT: THAT'S A PITY. 'SEDIMENTARY ROCK' COVERS A LOT OF TERRITORY. THERE ARE ALL SORTS OF INTERESTING SEDIMENTARY ROCKS, AND IT MIGHT HAVE BEEN INTERESTING TO SEE WHAT SORT THIS ONE WAS. GEOLOGY IS SORT OF A HOBBY OF MINE.

BUT I SUPPOSE IT IS OFF THE POINT IN THIS CASE. PLEASE CONTINUE, MS. BARRON.

MS. BARRON: DR. MAYRICK, WILL YOU TELL US SPECIFICALLY WHAT LED YOU TO BELIEVE A BLOW TO THE HEAD WAS THE CAUSE OF DEATH?

THE WITNESS: WELL, THE CALVARIUM REVEALED BY THE TORN SCALP SHOWED SIGNS THAT—

THE COURT: EXCUSE ME, MS. BARRON, IS THIS NEXT SECTION OF TESTIMONY GOING TO BE A TECHNICAL EXPLANATION OF THE AUTOPSY FINDINGS?

MS. BARRON: YES, YOUR HONOR.

THE COURT: THEN IF NEITHER COUNSEL HAS ANY OBJECTION, I THINK THIS WOULD BE A GOOD TIME TO TAKE A SHORT RECESS. I'VE GOT A SHORT-CAUSE MOTION ON CALENDAR FOR SOME TIME THIS AFTERNOON, AND I'D LIKE TO GET IT TAKEN CARE OF. IT WILL

ALSO GIVE US A CHANCE TO FORTIFY OURSELVES AGAINST A BEWILDERING SPECIAL TERMINOLOGY. ALL RIGHT?

    MR. RANDALL: FINE, YOUR HONOR.

    MS. BARRON: VERY WELL.

    THE COURT: WE'LL START AGAIN IN FIFTEEN MINUTES.

13

After the judge had left the courtroom, Randall leaned over and whispered to Kolvek, "Let's take a little walk."

Their walk was silent until they got outside: Randall had warned Kolvek not to talk about the case in the courtroom or the courtroom hallways, because neither place was really private.

They sat down on a bench on the courthouse grounds. "Do you want a cup of coffee?" Randall asked. Kolvek shook his head. "Now. Any questions about this afternoon?"

"I don't understand what all that was about whether or not Sharon came home that night."

"Okay. What I'm trying to do is poke away at the weak spots in their case; I want to see how they shore it up. If they can't put your wife in the house again that night, they're going to have a tough time convincing a jury that you're the one most likely to have killed her.

"But what they'll probably do is put the officer on the stand who took the missing persons report. He'll say you told him that some of her possessions had been removed. Now the most reasonable explanation for their disappearance is that she came back and got them. The other alternative is that whoever killed her broke into the house in the middle of the night and took them. That's possible, of course. But it presumes that you didn't hear the break-in. And no locks or windows were broken.

"But our biggest problem is that they seem to have a witness who will say she saw someone carrying a large bundle out of your house that night, out to the car. I have to find out how much weight they're giving that testimony. What we really want is someone who saw her alive away from the house some time after — say — four o'clock Wednesday morning. That would give her time to get back to the house, pack and leave again. Unfortunately we haven't been able to find anybody like that. That doesn't mean it didn't happen.

"She came back, either alone or with her killer, and left again. Or she never came back and her killer was somebody with access to the house. Or her killer was somebody working with someone with access to the house. The possibilities are endless, as long as the prosecution can't specifically put her alive in your house at one moment and dead the next.

I want to make sure they can't. I want to force them into a corner where they have to show me all the cards they're holding.

"We were lucky to get Judge Estevez as a prelim judge. He runs a very loose hearing, so we're getting a lot of information we probably wouldn't get with another judge. We have to get all the information we need, and at the same time keep the prosecution from getting too much on the record that we don't want on there. So I've been throwing in a few objections just to keep them on their toes. Is everything clear?"

"I guess so," Kolvek said. After a moment he said hesitantly, "There's just one other thing."

Randall picked up his briefcase and looked at him.

"It's about Elaine."

"Your daughter? What about her?"

"She just sits there in the courtroom and glares at me the whole time. I suppose you can't do anything about it, but it can't be making too good an impression on the judge."

"I didn't notice. I really don't think the judge is going to be influenced by it, but if it's bothering you we can take care of it." He looked at his watch. "We're going to have to scramble. Time's almost up."

They walked quickly back to the courthouse and to the fourth floor courtroom, where Randall went to the defense table and pulled out a file. He began to riffle through it rapidly. "I know Sally must have put a blank one in here somewhere, if I can just find it — ahah!" He pulled a subpoena from the file and scribbled in Elaine Morris's name and the date. He went into the spectator section and handed the paper to Elaine Morris, turning back to the defense table before she had a chance to say anything to him. He reached his chair just as the clerk came in and announced the judge's entrance.

When the judge had settled into his chair everybody sat down except Randall. "Was there something you wanted to say before we get back into Dr Mayrick's testimony, Mr Randall?"

"Yes, your Honor. I wanted to renew my motion to exclude witnesses."

Judge Estevez looked surprised. "I don't see why you'd want to renew it. I granted your motion for the whole course of the preliminary hearing. But if you want me to restate it, I will. All individuals who have been subpoenaed to testify in this matter are instructed to wait outside the courtroom until called, and are further instructed not to discuss this case with each other. The sole exception is Mr Janis, as the investigating officer."

Randall heard several thuds behind him; he did not need to turn to identify them as emanating from Elaine Morris, who was gathering her possessions together as noisily as she could, to express her outrage at this frustration of her intentions. Randall grinned to himself as he heard the door swish shut behind her. He had intended to call her to the stand anyway. It wouldn't hurt her to have to sit and stew for a while outside the courtroom.

TRANSCRIPT OF PRELIMINARY HEARING

PEOPLE OF THE STATE OF CALIFORNIA

vs. JOSEPH WILLIAM KOLVEK

COUNTY OF SAN MARIN, STATE OF CALIFORNIA

Wednesday, November 13, 1985 — Morning Session: 8:49 a.m.

THE COURT: THE PEOPLE VERSUS JOSEPH KOLVEK. THE COURT FINDS THE DEFENDANT PRESENT WITH HIS ATTORNEY, JAMES RANDALL, AND THE PEOPLE'S COUNSEL, ELIZABETH BARRON, ALSO PRESENT.

EVERYBODY, LET'S TRY TO MOVE THIS HEARING ALONG. THIS PROCEEDING SHOULD HAVE ONLY TAKEN A COUPLE OF DAYS, AND WE'RE STARTING OUR THIRD DAY NOW WITH NO END IN SIGHT.

AS I REMEMBER, THE LAST WITNESS YESTERDAY AFTERNOON WAS THE POLICE OFFICER FROM THE MISSING PERSONS DIVISION.

MS. BARRON: THAT'S CORRECT, YOUR HONOR.

THE COURT: AND WE WERE THROUGH WITH HIM?

MR. RANDALL: I HAD NO FURTHER QUESTIONS OF HIM, YOUR HONOR.

MS. BARRON: THE PEOPLE HAD NO FURTHER QUESTIONS.

THE COURT: THEN LET'S MOVE ON.

MS. BARRON: THE PEOPLE CALL ALYDIA MICHAELS TO THE STAND.

ALYDIA MICHAELS,
HAVING BEEN CALLED AS A WITNESS BY AND ON BEHALF OF THE PEOPLE, AND HAVING BEEN FIRST DULY SWORN, WAS EXAMINED AND TESTIFIED AS FOLLOWS:

MS. BARRON: WOULD YOU GIVE US YOUR FULL NAME, PLEASE, AND SPELL YOUR LAST NAME?

THE WITNESS: ALYDIA MICHAELS, M-I-C-H-A-E-L-S.

Q: PERHAPS YOU'D BETTER SPELL YOUR FIRST NAME FOR THE REPORTER, ALSO.

A: A-L-Y-D-I-A.

Q: WHAT IS YOUR RESIDENCE ADDRESS, PLEASE, MS. MICHAELS?

A: IT'S MRS. MICHAELS. I LIVE AT 13135 REYNA WAY.

Q: HOW LONG HAVE YOU LIVED AT THAT ADDRESS?

A: SINCE THE HOUSE WAS BUILT, ABOUT SIX YEARS.

Q: AND HOW LONG HAVE YOU BEEN NEIGHBORS WITH THE KOLVEKS?

MR. RANDALL: OBJECTION. NO FOUNDATION.

THE COURT: SUSTAINED.

MS. BARRON: MS. MICHAELS, DO YOU KNOW THE NUMBER OF THE HOUSE NEXT TO YOURS?

THE WITNESS: IT'S MRS. MICHAELS. THE HOUSE NEXT TO US IS 13127 REYNA WAY.

Q: AND DO YOU KNOW WHO LIVES THERE?

A: JOSEPH AND SHARON KOLVEK. OR RATHER, JUST JOSEPH KOLVEK NOW.

Q: AND HOW LONG HAVE YOU BEEN NEIGHBORS WITH THE KOLVEKS?

A: AS LONG AS WE'VE LIVED THERE, OR ALMOST. THEY MOVED IN ABOUT TWO MONTHS AFTER WE DID.

Q: SO YOU KNOW MR. KOLVEK VERY WELL BY SIGHT?

MR. RANDALL: OBJECTION. LEADING.

THE COURT: I'M GOING TO SUSTAIN THAT, BUT YOU MIGHT REMEMBER, MR. RANDALL, THAT THIS IS JUST A PRELIMINARY HEARING. THERE'S NO NEED TO BE QUITE SO TECHNICAL ABOUT EVERYTHING.

REPHRASE THE QUESTION, PLEASE, MS. BARRON.

MS. BARRON: YES, YOUR HONOR.

DO YOU KNOW MR. KOLVEK BY SIGHT?

THE WITNESS: YES. I'VE SEEN HIM ALMOST EVERY DAY, OR AT LEAST EVERY WEEKEND, FOR SIX YEARS.

Q: DO YOU SEE HIM HERE IN THIS COURTROOM?

A: YES. THAT MAN SITTING THERE.

THE COURT: LET THE RECORD REFLECT THE WITNESS HAS INDICATED THE DEFENDANT.

MS. BARRON: NOW, TURNING TO THE NIGHT OF TUESDAY, AUGUST 6, OR RATHER THE EARLY MORNING OF WEDNESDAY, AUGUST 7. DO YOU REMEMBER ANYTHING UNUSUAL HAPPENING THAT NIGHT?

THE WITNESS: YES. I WAS RESTLESS THAT NIGHT, AND I WENT DOWN TO THE KITCHEN TO GET A GLASS OF MILK. WHEN I CAME BACK UPSTAIRS TO THE BEDROOM, I WALKED OVER TO THE BEDROOM, I WALKED OVER TO THE WINDOW TO DRINK MY MILK THERE.

Q: DO YOU REMEMBER WHAT TIME IT WAS?

A: IT WAS ABOUT 3:15, MAYBE 3:30.

Q: CONTINUE, PLEASE.

A: AS I WAS STANDING THERE, I NOTICED SOME MOVEMENT DOWN BY THE KOLVEKS' GARAGE. I KEPT WATCHING, AND I SAW A LARGE FIGURE CARRYING SEVERAL SMALL BUNDLES AND PUTTING THEM INTO THE BACK SEAT OF A CAR THAT WAS SITTING THERE. AS I LOOKED, I SAW THE MAN MAKE ANOTHER TRIP, THIS TIME WITH A LARGER BUNDLE OVER HIS SHOULDER. HE PUT IT IN THE FRONT PASSENGER SEAT. HE WENT AWAY FOR A

WHILE, THEN HE CAME BACK AND GOT IN THE DRIVER'S SEAT OF THE CAR, AND DROVE AWAY.

Q: DO YOU KNOW WHAT SORT OF CAR IT WAS?

A: I'M NOT TOO GOOD WITH CARS, BUT I THINK IT WAS MRS. KOLVEK'S CHEVETTE.

Q: THANK YOU. THAT'S ALL I HAVE.

THE COURT: MR. RANDALL?

MR. RANDALL: THANK YOU, YOUR HONOR.

CROSS-EXAMINATION:

Q: FIRST OF ALL, MS. MICHAELS —

THE WITNESS: IT'S MRS. MICHAELS.

Q: I'M SORRY. MRS. MICHAELS. YOU REFER TO THE LARGE FIGURE BY USING A MASCULINE PRONOUN. WHY DID YOU THINK IT WAS A MAN?

A: THE WAY HE CARRIED THAT BIG BUNDLE SO EASILY. AND THE WAY HE MOVED.

Q: BUT YOU DIDN'T SPECIFICALLY SEE THAT IT WAS A MAN?

A: NO, I COULDN'T SEE ANY FEATURES AT ALL.

Q: SO IT COULD HAVE BEEN A STRONG WOMAN?

A: I DON'T THINK SO.

Q: BUT IT COULD HAVE BEEN?

A: (NO RESPONSE).

Q: AND EVEN IF THE FIGURE WERE A MAN, YOU COULD NOT TELL THAT IT WAS JOSEPH KOLVEK?

A: OH, NO. I NEVER SAID IT WAS, TO ANYBODY. I JUST SAW A LARGE FIGURE, MOVING AROUND.

Q: THAT BRINGS ME TO MY NEXT QUESTION. I HAVE BEEN TO THE KOLVEK HOUSE, AND CHECKED OUT HOW IT'S SITED IN RELATION TO YOUR HOUSE. ISN'T IT TRUE THERE ARE SEVERAL LARGE TREES IN THE FRONT OF THE KOLVEK YARD WHICH WOULD HAVE BLOCKED YOUR VIEW OF THE GARAGE AREA, AND ALSO THE CORNER OF HOUSE, GIVEN THE ANGLE AT WHICH YOU MUST HAVE BEEN LOOKING IF YOU WERE STANDING AT YOUR BEDROOM WINDOW — THE CORNER OF THE KOLVEK HOUSE WOULD HAVE IMPEDED YOUR VISION?

A: WELL, IT'S TRUE THAT I ONLY CAUGHT GLIMPSES OF THE FIGURE. I DIDN'T SEE WHERE IT WAS COMING FROM, I JUST SAW IT WHEN IT WAS ACTUALLY NEXT TO THE CAR.

Q: I HAVE CHECKED THE U.S. WEATHER SERVICE, MRS. MICHAELS, AND THEY SAY THAT NIGHT HAD POOR VISIBILITY DUE TO LOW-LYING CLOUDS. THE MOON WASN'T FULL AND IT MUST HAVE BEEN VERY DARK. HOW WAS IT YOU WERE ABLE TO SEE ANYTHING AT ALL?

A: WE LIVE IN A VERY WELL SECURED NEIGHBOR-HOOD. ALL THE HOUSES HAVE FLOODLIGHTS.

Q: AND YOU SPECIFICALLY RECALL THAT THE KOLVEK HOUSE WAS FLOODLIT THAT NIGHT?

A: WELL, IT MUST HAVE BEEN FOR ME TO SEE ANY-THING, IF AS YOU SAY IT WAS DARK THAT NIGHT.

Q: BUT YOU DON'T HAVE ANY SPECIFIC RECOL-LECTION?

A: NO.

Q: ONE LAST QUESTION, MRS. MICHAELS. YOU SEEM VERY SURE ABOUT THE DATE AND THE TIME, BUT THAT WAS THREE MONTHS AGO. HOW CAN YOU BE SO CER-TAIN THIS ALL OCCURRED ON AUGUST 6/7?

A: AS I SAID, I WAS RESTLESS THAT NIGHT. THE REASON I WAS RESTLESS WAS BECAUSE MY DAUGHTER WAS DUE TO GIVE BIRTH TO MY FIRST GRANDCHILD AT ANY TIME. I WAS CONCERNED FOR HER. AND AS IT HAPPENS SHE WENT INTO LABOR ABOUT 8:00 THE NEXT MORNING AND GAVE ME A GRANDDAUGHTER ABOUT 10:00 THAT NIGHT. THAT'S A PRETTY GOOD WAY TO HAVE A DATE STICK IN YOUR MIND.

(LAUGHTER IN THE COURTROOM.)

Q: YES, I SUPPOSE YOU WOULD REMEMBER

SOMETHING LIKE THAT. CAN YOU TELL ME WHY, WHEN THE OFFICER INVESTIGATING THE MISSING PERSONS REPORT ON SHARON KOLVEK CAME AROUND TO ASK IF YOU'D SEEN ANYTHING, YOU DIDN'T TELL HIM ANYTHING ABOUT THIS?

A: I SUPPOSE I JUST FORGOT. IT WAS A PRETTY HECTIC TIME FOR ALL OF US, AND I JUST DIDN'T REMEMBER UNTIL MR. JANIS FROM THE DISTRICT ATTORNEY'S OFFICE CAME AND WENT OVER THE WHOLE EVENING WITH ME CAREFULLY.

Q: BUT ANOTHER INVESTIGATOR, A PRIVATE INVESTIGATOR, CAME AROUND AFTER MR. JANIS, AND YOU DIDN'T TELL HER ANYTHING EITHER.

A: NO. AS I REMEMBER I HAD SOME WORKMEN PUTTING UP WALLPAPER THAT DAY AND I JUST DIDN'T HAVE TIME TO TALK. SO I TOLD HER I DIDN'T KNOW ANYTHING.

Q: I SEE. NO FURTHER QUESTIONS.

THE COURT: ANYTHING ON REDIRECT, MS. BARRON?

MS. BARRON: NO, YOUR HONOR.

THE COURT: THEN YOU'RE EXCUSED, MRS. MICHAELS. THANK YOU.

14

"How did it go?" Sally asked. She noticed Randall's expression. "Never mind," she said hastily.

"Let's just say their side got in a few good licks this morning," Randall said. He motioned Kolvek to go ahead of him into his office and followed him in. He put his briefcase on the desk and sank into his swivel chair.

"Well," he said, after a few minutes of silence, "Mrs Michaels just booted any remote chance we had for a dismissal right out the door. Of course I saw the reports on her story when the D.A. handed over the discovery, but somehow I didn't think she'd be that strong as a witness. You see, our problem is that the prosecutors aren't looking at any suspects but you, and we haven't been able to turn up anything to convince them to change their direction. We need something surefire; we're working on it. We could turn it up any day.

"The People haven't proved you did it by any means, but I do think they've shown enough so that the judge is going to say that a jury will have to decide the issue. I'll make a *pro forma* motion for dismissal, but it won't go anywhere."

"What's that mean?"

"What? *Pro forma?* It means it's just a formality. I'm just making the motion to preserve the record, but I don't think it's got a chance of flying. Now I don't want you to think this means you won't have a prayer at trial. As I said, they're a long way from proving anything. All they've done is show reasonable cause to believe you *might* have done it. But even at that, they haven't shown any evidence at all of premeditation.

"I don't think they're going to have any surprises for us in the afternoon session, and they'll probably rest after that. Then I'll make my motion to dismiss, which will undoubtedly be denied, and then we'll put our case on the stand. That's just basically going to consist of putting Evans Jake on, so we can find out what he's got to say, and then I'll put the charge slips signed with your wife's name into evidence so the judge will know there's a valid reason why you weren't concerned about her being missing."

"How bad was Mrs Michaels' testimony?"

"It's hard to tell. But I don't think it'll be as bad with a jury at a trial as it was with the judge. There's a lot of flack when cases are dismissed at the preliminary hearing stage. Estevez is a good, fair judge, but we're not giving him anything to go on. That's why I went easy on Mrs Michaels; it wouldn't have made any difference at this point.

"But with a jury it will make a difference. There are a lot of weaknesses in her story. I already brought out the fact that she didn't even know whether the figure she saw was a man or a woman. She wasn't even sure what car it was. And what was the big bundle? The assumption is that it was your wife's body, but an assumption is not proof. And then on top of everything else, was Mrs Michaels wearing her glasses that night? Did she put her glasses on just to get a glass of milk?"

"That's right," Kolvek said. "I do remember she usually wears glasses. But how did you know?"

Randall shrugged. "I saw the marks on the bridge of her nose. But I'm just showing you how weak her testimony really is. And the D.A. is putting a lot of weight on it, because she's the closest thing they have to an eyewitness."

"You mentioned those trees in my front yard would really have blocked her view," Kolvek said.

Randall nodded. "Yes. I just threw that in. To tell you the truth I'm not sure—I'd have to go into her house and look out her window..."

He rose. "So we start again at one-thirty. Why don't you go ahead and grab some lunch and be back here at one-fifteen and we'll walk over to the courthouse together. In the meantime I want to take a quick look at my mail. I've got a couple of feelers still out — tests being run... who knows, the final bit of evidence to solve this might be on Sally's desk right this minute."

When Kolvek had left, Sally said, "You've got a couple of telephone messages that you should get to before you go back to court, if you can. There's not much in the mail except a letter from Roger Higgins. I can't make anything out of it — it's about some rocks."

Randall flipped through his telephone messages and took the mail from her absently. He wandered back into his office, thinking about the calls he had to return; one in particular was rather troublesome. He sat down and punched out the numbers written on the message slip. While the phone rang he scanned the letter from Roger quickly and put it down. After a second he picked it up again and looked at it once more. Dimly he heard a voice on the line saying "Hello?" and then on a rising note of irritation, "Hello? Hello?"

He put the receiver back on the cradle.

He read the letter once more, carefully, and then said, clearly, "God damn it." He sat for a moment and then said it again, slowly. It didn't help.

He called Sally. She came in, looking at him anxiously. "What happened? What's wrong?"

"Go find Kolvek," he snapped. "I need him back here right now."

She opened her mouth to ask where in the world she could find Kolvek with all of downtown to look in, but Randall's expression made her think better of the question. Prudently she vanished.

Slowly Randall got up from his chair and walked over to the window. He stared out, unseeing.

ROGER HIGGINS, Ph.D., F.G.S.A.
Registered Geologist

Jim --

We've been missing each other on the phone, so I thought I'd send off a quick note to let you know my preliminary findings on those particles you sent me.

They are indeed from a rock of sedimentary origin, but that's something like describing a human being just by saying "a mammal." Sedimentary rocks cover about seventy-five percent of the surface land area of the earth, as you would have remembered if you'd had your mind on geology in class instead of that blonde in front of you.

Anyway, these particular fragments are of sandstone. Specifically, a pink, medium-grained sandstone which is a good aquifer. You told me you didn't want any detailed mineralogical description, just a layman's description, so I'll leave it at that.

With the very minute sample you gave me, I couldn't give you any idea from the sediments themselves where the rock might have come from. However, we lucked out. Embedded in one of the larger particles was a fragment of shell. I took it to a friend of mine and she says it's part of a Mooreoceras, sp. aff. M. cliftonense. Now you know as much as you did before, right?

Well, Mooreoceras is an ancient cephalopod, more particularly a nautiloid. What that means to you is it's a relative of that modern shell I'm sure you've seen, the spiraled Nautilus.

What's the point? The point is that, though found elsewhere, this particular shell is a trademark of an old sandstone quarry located in lower Michigan. Specifically, in Marshall, Michigan. In case you don't have an atlas, that's in Calhoun County. The nearest large city is Battle Creek. The quarry is abandoned now, but the rocks from it were used in a lot of structures in the area, and who knows where they went from there. So maybe that's not so much help after all, huh? But it was incredible I was able to narrow it down even that much for you. Quite a stroke of luck, huh?

If you need a formal report on this, let me know and I'll tart it up for you. Are you going to be at the alma mater's alumni game? I'll keep an eye peeled for you if you are. You bring your flask and I'll bring mine.

Fraternally,
Roger

15

Randall wondered why he was so shocked: the odds had always been in favor of Kolvek having killed his wife.

But he had come to like Kolvek, and he had thought he understood him, at least a little. He liked the man's patience and willingness to accept advice; he admired his dignity and his refusal to whine and complain about the hard knocks that he had had.

And as the case progressed Randall had come to see it as a kind of jigsaw puzzle, where the pieces were being doled out a few at a time. It had been a busy puzzle, with many pieces. and now just one piece had come in that had brought the whole puzzle together; the pieces that were still missing were really superfluous. At the heart of the picture were just Joseph and Sharon Kolvek.

Randall picked up the geologist's report once more. Almost automatically he swore at Higgins for putting his findings in writing when he had specifically told him not to. But his heart wasn't in it. It didn't really matter. The report put the murder weapon firmly into Joseph Kolvek's hands. And even if Higgins had not made a discoverable report, the chances were good that Elizabeth Barron would have picked up on Judge Estevez's casual suggestion that she have the rock fragments analyzed. And if Randall's tiny fragment contained the telltale fossil, so undoubtedly would the much larger segment being held by the coroner's office.

From there it would be a small step for Elizabeth to realize that the one person in the case most likely to have rocks from Calhoun County was Joseph Kolvek. Then she would get a search warrant and find the fireplace and the pool surround. He could still remember Kolvek standing at the pool, saying that it was one of the few things in the house which he had built himself. That and the fireplace.

Five minutes later Sally nervously ushered Kolvek into the office and withdrew, shutting the door behind her.

"Sit down, Mr Kolvek," Randall said. "I have something here that you have to look at."

He handed him the letter.

Kolvek read it through very slowly. Then he looked up at Randall. Their eyes met.

"I don't understand," Kolvek said.

"Well," Randall said, "I'll try to explain it to you then. Now, at the time of the autopsy I requested portions of samples taken from your wife's body for independent analysis — that means I wanted my own experts to examine these things. Blood samples, tissue samples, hair samples. There were also some particles of rock material which had been vacuumed from the wound. The assumption was that a rock had been used to kill her and a rock was in fact established as the murder weapon. A rock. You know that. I sent all the samples to specialists, asking for informal analyses. And this report came from the geologist — the specialist who studied the rock particles. Do you follow?"

Kolvek stared at him, and shook his head. "No. I don't understand."

Randall took a deep breath. "Mr Kolvek. Look. Because of these rock particles — taken from your wife's head wound — the prosecution can show that it is highly likely that only you had access to the murder weapon. I can't swear that they can get over the reasonable doubt standard, but there is a definite chance that they can, with this evidence. Up to now I really think they were fishing."

Kolvek remained silent and impassive.

"Are you following now?" Randall said impatiently. "Do you understand that the situation has completely changed?"

"I've told you," Kolvek said quietly. "I don't understand."

Randall could feel his temper going. "Don't understand! It couldn't be clearer — " He stopped. "You're saying you don't know what the geologist's report means," he said, in a controlled voice.

"I don't know what any of it means," Kolvek said. "All I know is you're telling me that they think I killed Sharon. But I knew that before." His stolidity seemed to become more pronounced as he felt himself under attack.

"There was a fossil fragment in particles of rock retrieved from the wound which resulted in your wife's death. That particular fossil is found almost exclusively in an abandoned sandstone quarry in Calhoun County, Michigan. Where you grew up."

"A fossil fragment," Kolvek repeated. "A fossil—part of an animal that died a long time ago?"

"That's right."

An expression of incredulity flitted for an instant over Kolvek's face. Not fear or concern. "You're telling me," he said, "that they know where the rock came from because they found part of a dead animal in it?" He paused and thought about it for a moment. "That's just foolishness," he said firmly.

"Mr Kolvek," Randall said. "These are sciences—paleontology, geology. Believe me, the technique is widely used and respected. You have to take my word for it. Unfortunately for you, this particular fossil is rare. Most fossils are scattered all over the country, but this one pinpoints Calhoun

County, Michigan. And the weapon has been pretty much put into your hands."

"But what about all the stuff you turned up? That man in the bar... and Thomas wasn't home that night... The bartender... Credit cards—"

"That's all irrelevant now. Right now I have evidence here that the prosecution will surely use as the final link in a chain that started when you went back to Michigan to close up your father's estate and brought some of those rocks back with you. And you used them at your house, to build your fireplace and your pool surround."

He looked at Kolvek. "I need a completely honest answer from you. Is that what you did? Did you bring those rocks back to California with you? And did this rock come from your old farm house?"

"Yes," Kolvek said. "It was from the old wall."

Randall nodded. He had expected the truth from Kolvek. It appeared now that the man was a murderer, but he was not a liar. Or was he really the murderer? Other people may have had access to those rocks... But the rocks had been carefully placed and mortared. Kolvek was a meticulous worker; he would immediately notice any alteration in his work. Unless he made the alteration himself.

"If Elizabeth Barron discovers this

information," Randall said, "I think she will use it to convict you of premeditated first-degree murder. So our primary concern right now is what we're going to do about this." He lifted Roger Higgins' letter from the desk and let it float back down again.

"Well," Kolvek said, "this stuff is supposed to prove that I killed Sharon. And you're right. I did. So I guess you'll want me to be leaving now."

He rose from his chair.

"Hey, wait!" Randall said. "You can't go now. We've got some decisions to make."

Kolvek sat down again. "What decisions? You say they've got me dead to rights."

"Without an eyewitness who says he saw someone else handling the murder weapon, the prosecution has a good chance to prove beyond a reasonable doubt that only you had custody and control of the weapon. The scales have tipped against us. And there is no such eyewitness, is there?"

It crossed his mind that Margaret Walters may have been trying to tell him that she was willing to perjure herself if necessary to save Kolvek. Possibly she knew he was guilty. It didn't matter. She — or they — had picked the wrong lawyer for that.

Kolvek hesitated, and then shook his head slowly. "No, I don't know of any witnesses like that."

"So we have to keep all this in mind when we make our decisions."

Kolvek looked at him with a kind of faint curiosity. "You don't seem very upset; I just told you I killed my wife."

Randall shrugged. "Well, I knew you did when I read the letter. I didn't ask you about it. Now we've got to deal with this evidence. Right now Elizabeth Barron doesn't know about it. But we have to assume that she will know about it before very long. So we have to decide what action we're going to take."

"I thought as soon as you knew I killed Sharon you would refuse to be my lawyer any more."

"Mr Kolvek," Randall said, "it would be unprofessional for me to desert you at this crucial time, just because new evidence has surfaced. I'm afraid most of my clients are guilty of something; that's the sad fact. Now I don't know whether you killed your wife in the heat of passion or whether you planned the murder. At this moment my job is to protect your rights. Your guilt or innocence will be decided by a jury, not by me.

"Now as I see it, you have two choices. One, we can go to trial despite this new information. We can hope that Elizabeth Barron won't get the information or that if she does, the jury will not find it convincing." He looked at Kolvek as an idea struck him. "Maybe we could prove that there were some loose rocks left over after you finished your work and someone else could have gotten hold of them."

Kolvek shook his head. Of course, no careful workman would leave loose rocks lying around. It was unthinkable.

"Okay," Randall said. He sighed faintly. "So what I am saying is that one option is for us to continue to act defensively, to hold our cards close to our chests and wait for the prosecutor to play hers. We can wait for her moves before we react.

"Or our other choice is to go on the offensive. I can ask Elizabeth what she would do if hypothetically we were willing to plead to involuntary manslaughter right now. It would probably mean that you would have to do some time, but not nearly as much as you would if she were able to get a conviction even of voluntary manslaughter. And remember, she's not going after voluntary manslaughter, she's going to be trying for first-degree murder."

"What do you think I should do?"

"I've given you the options," Randall said. "I think we have a shot at acquittal if we go to trial. But it's risky and if we fail you're facing a lot harder fall than if she will go for a plea now. Of course if we make this offer she's going to suspect that something is up ... but then she has always believed you were guilty."

Kolvek stared at Randall; he was clearly deep in thought. He looked as impassive as always. He could have been considering making a bid to build an addition to Randall's house. In this situation Randall had had clients who wept, or raged, or protested their innocence. But Kolvek continued to play the hand he was dealt. And now he was slowly deciding his next move. To look at him, no one would guess that the rest of his life was on the line.

"I don't go for the long shots," he said calmly. "Do what you can about the deal."

Randall felt a fleeting pang of regret for the spectacular trial that could have been. But now his task as Joseph Kolvek's lawyer was to protect his client as well as he could from the consequences of his own actions.

He dialed Elizabeth Barron's number. The mystery was solved. The legal consequences were just beginning.

BEFORE

He stood staring down at the body of the woman who, years ago, had been his wife. He had not called Sharon his wife for a very long time. He did not think of her that way any more.

He went back to the pool and carefully repositioned the rock, making sure it was properly aligned. He would remortar it tomorrow. No one would look at the pool for a murder weapon, but the rock belonged in a certain place and it should be there.

When he finished he went into the house and upstairs to the bedroom, where he neatly packed up those possessions of Sharon's which she would most likely take with her on a trip.

When he carried the suitcases out to her car, he noticed that as usual she had parked it partially on the lawn. She wouldn't be doing that any more. It was hurting the grass. He tossed the bags into the back seat; they could be stolen more easily from there than from the trunk.

He went back and picked up the body, carrying it easily to the front seat of the car. Her head struck the door frame. That was all right. She was just 125 pounds of inert matter. He slammed the car door and went back to the house to check the living room and bedroom for anything he might have forgotten. Sure enough, her handbag was on the table in the entry hall. He took it with him and left the house, carefully locking the door and making sure that the outside spotlights were on. This was a low crime area, but it didn't do to be careless about burglars.

He got into the Chevette and started it up. It was idling too high; he had told Sharon a thousand times to take better care of that car. He had thought for some time that she neglected things on purpose just to irritate him. Slowly he pulled out of the driveway and started down the dark streets. Once he was on the freeway he picked up speed, but stayed under fifty-five miles an hour. He was proud of his driving record; he had never had a speeding ticket.

He ran quickly over his plans. He knew the spot where he would pull over and take the body a little way into the woods, leaving it in a ditch with no attempt to bury it at all. With any luck it would not be found until well on in the fall when it would not be easy to tell what had happened to it. If it were found earlier it would just look as though she had been wandering around drunk and had tripped over something and fallen.

After he dropped off the body he would drive the car a little further into the trees and leave it, with Sharon's purse and suitcases inside. It would be stripped before the month was out, and the odds were that whoever stripped it would use Sharon's credit cards, further muddying the waters. He had decided against using her cards a few times himself on some short trips away from home. He really didn't have time for that. This way was better, although unfortunately it would cost him money for someone else's bills. He just hoped they would not carry it to extremes.

He could easily walk home. It was no more than twenty-five miles, not that bad. He had walked miles to school every morning, sometimes in the snow.

He liked the idea that he had used the rock from the wall around the house that Sharon had hated so much. It served her right. She always felt she was meant for better things, but when he finally made it she was never able to fit in. She wanted all the benefits but she never wanted to pay for them. He had known long before he met Margaret that Sharon was an albatross around his neck; he had known from the first Association dinner party that something would have to be done about her. He considered divorce, even though he did not approve of it. But he knew that he would never be rid of Sharon that way. If he had learned one thing in life, it was to cut himself off completely from things he was through with.

So this was the only way. Now he could marry Margaret and with her co-operation he could achieve what he wanted. He didn't need money any longer; he wanted independence and respect. He deserved it.

And he wanted a son. He had had to accept Thomas, even though he knew from the first that the boy was not his. He never said a word to Sharon and simply stared at her when she hinted around. He had had no other options. Now he did. Margaret was barely forty. She could still have children; she had two attractive sons from her first marriage. It was time for another Kolvek to come along to take over when he left off. And this one would be called Joseph, after him.

It was all going to work out. He had planned it, waiting for a night when all the elements were in place. He ran over the whole thing once more. He had thought of everything. Carefully he turned the car into the side road leading to the cabin.